TOXIC CANDY

TALES OF SUSPENSE, FANTASY, & HORROR

by Weldon Burge

Smart Rhino
Publications
www.smartrhino.com

"The Old Man on the Porch," *Dark & Stormy: An Anthology of Horror* (Archer Publishing, 2023).

"A Day at the Beach with the GramthrottleMax Family," *Beach Pulp* (Cat & Mouse Press, 2019).

"On the Viaduct," *Scary Stuff* (Oddity Prodigy Productions, 2020).

"Nanimwé," *Monster Fight at the O.K. Corral* (Tule Fog Press, 2023).

"The Last Hooky," *GlassFire Magazine* (Pegleg Publishing, 2007).

"Melvin & the Haunted Mansion," *Beach Nights* (Cat & Mouse Press, 2016).

"A Less-Than-Gratifying Vacation in Paris," *Suspense Magazine* (Suspense Publishing, 2021).

"Deerman," *Asinine Assassins* (Smart Rhino Publications, 2021).

"Hearing Mildred," *Zippered Flesh: Tales of Body Enhancements Gone Bad!* (Smart Rhino Publications, 2012).

"Jason Tries Online Dating," *Creatures, Crimes & Creativity 2019 Anthology* (Intrigue Publishing, 2019).

"Blue Eye Burn," *Out & About* (TSN Media, 2004).

"Welcome to the Food Chain," *Uncommon Assassins* (Smart Rhino Publications, 2012).

"Right-Hand Man," *Someone Wicked: A Written Remains Anthology* (Smart Rhino Publications, 2013).

"Vindictive," *A Plague of Shadows: A Written Remains Anthology* (Smart Rhino Publications, 2018).

ISBN-13: 979-8-9880625-3-0

Praise for Toxic Candy

"It might be *Toxic Candy*, but it's one helluva treat! In this story collection, Weldon Burge serves up a smorgasbord of lost souls, shapeshifters, killer deer, hitmen, and sea monsters, sauteed in thrills and a big dollop of humor. This is a *killer* collection, in more ways than one. C'mon, treat yourself!"
— L.L. Soares, Award-Winning Author of *Teach Them How to Bleed* and *Something Blue (And Other Colorful Deaths)*

"Burge paints vivid pictures in this collection of stories, which range from nostalgic to whimsical. Visceral images leavened with humor and bittersweet memories make for a satisfying collection."
— J. Gregory Smith, Author of the *Reluctant Hustler* series

"*Toxic Candy* is a dark ride through the depths of the human (and not so human) experience. Weldon has reached into the shadows of imagination, harkening to the likes of Bradbury and Matheson to bring the reader some of the best short stories I've read in a long time."
—Shaun Meeks, Author of *A Touch of Death*

"With everything from monsters to noir, from shapeshifters to sweet nostalgia and more, Weldon Burge's *Toxic Candy* has it all! No better way to spend an evening. Bravo!"
— Carson Buckingham, Author of *Too Late for Prayin'*

"These finely observed stories contain just the right balance of wit, insight, and terror. But what makes them truly horrifying is the humanity with which each of the characters is imbued."
— Jasper Bark, Author of *Stuck on You*

"Weldon Burge's *Toxic Candy* is a trick-or-treat bag full of chills, shivers, and creeps. Grab your flashlight, climb into your secret treehouse fort, dig in and get ready to shudder ... and giggle."
— JM Reinbold, Author of *Missing: A DCI Rylan Crowe Mystery*

CONTENTS

ACKNOWLEDGMENTS

Thanks go to the many publications and editors I've worked with over the years, who have graciously published my work. And, of course, thanks to my wife, Cindy, and my two sons, Chris and Eric, for their continued support.

THE OLD MAN ON THE PORCH

"Just leave him alone, Noah," his mother said. She didn't even look up from the eggs she scrambled in a pan on the stove. "I don't want you going near him."

Noah was eight at the time. He glanced out the window at the old man on the porch at the house across the way, the only other house on the stretch of land his family owned. His father had always hoped to develop the land, to build a true homestead in South Australia, just north of the Musgrave Ranges. His plan was to purchase more sheep and make the family business more profitable. But the dry, desert-like conditions and adjoining mountains made that nearly impossible. The plan died when he did.

The elderly man sat in a rocking chair, and Noah had never seen him move from it. The man looked to be hundreds of years old, his face lined with crevices, skin as pale as milk. On his head was one tuft of stark-white hair, growing like a mushroom from his scalp.

"Who is he, Ma?" Noah asked, not for the first time.

His mother merely shook her head. She turned from the stove and shoveled a mound of eggs on his plate. "Never you mind," she said. The answer he always got to the question. "I just don't want to see you near him."

"How long has he been there?" Another frequent question.

She looked out the window. "Probably since the start of time." Then she turned back to him. "But never you mind. Just stay away from him, you hear?"

And that was the first time Noah recognized fear behind her eyes.

* * *

For years, he followed his mother's advice, keeping his distance from the man who perpetually rocked on the porch not a hundred yards from Noah's home. He never understood how the man's home never changed, never seemed to deteriorate despite the lack of maintenance. How the man apparently never ate or drank, never needed sleep. Like an addiction, curiosity drove Noah to learn more.

One day, when his parents had traveled to the town of Oodnadatta to purchase supplies and food to stock their pantry, he steeled his nerves to address the man. When Noah approached the front step of the porch, the man stopped rocking. But he didn't look at him, just stared at the horizon, no expression on his face.

Noah had never seen the man stop rocking before.

He put one foot on the step, and the man looked down at him. The man's eyes were pupil-less, pure gray. Maybe he was blind. His eyes didn't blink. Noah couldn't tell if he was staring at him or was just aware of his presence.

"Mister …" Noah suddenly didn't know what to say, his questions evaporating in his mind. Why was he here in the first place? Mere curiosity? Or did he want to conquer his fear of the man?

The man cocked his head, almost mechanically, and his seemingly sightless eyes widened. When was the last time anyone had spoken to him?

"Mister, are you okay?" Dumb question, but the only thing that came to Noah's mind.

He stepped back from the porch. Why had he done this, despite his mother's warnings?

The old man smiled, but something far from a human smile. A bizarre curving of the lips, the corners of his mouth nearly reaching his ears.

He winked at Noah.

Noah ran.

* * *

When Noah became a teenager, he worked with his father, tending to the sheep and the small garden they had behind their home—a futile attempt to raise their own food in the brutal desert climate of the outback. Noah half-expected the vegetables to burst into flame on any particularly fiery afternoon.

One day, while mending a fence a ram had broken during the night, Noah noticed how gnarled and calloused his father's hands were, the knuckles swollen and bruised. He then looked at his own hands. Not as severely damaged as his father's hands from years of hard labor, but calloused with broken nails. Noah wondered if this was the life he genuinely wanted.

As his father replaced a broken fence rail, Noah turned to stare at the old man.

"Stop staring at him," his father said without looking up from his work. "There's no sense staring. Nothing changes."

"Pa, who is he? I mean, really? Who is he?"

Noah's father shook his head. "I don't know what the thing is."

Thing. Not a man. Thing.

"It's not human," his father continued. "We don't know what it is. But it has been here as long as our family has owned this land."

"Ma said he's always been here."

"Our ancestors owned and respected this land for generations. That thing has been on that parcel for probably centuries, who knows? Some say he sat on a boulder long, long ago, always facing east. No one knows when the house appeared. An old man, rocking in that chair, never standing, never eating, never sleeping. Just rocking and gazing out over the desert like it's waiting for something. Makes no sense."

"How is that possible? To live that long?"

"It's not. At least not for regular folk. Or any living thing."

"Why haven't we moved away from here, then?"

His father shook his head again. "Your grandfather and his father, and the fathers before, lived on this land. It's our history, our heritage." He pointed at the old man. "That thing will not drive us from our homestead."

Noah said nothing, not wishing to disagree with his Pa. But he was convinced that the man on the porch didn't care what they did. He understood his father's pride in the land and his love for their family and its legacy. But it meant nothing to the old man staring into the distance.

Noah's father often talked with him about their Aboriginal ancestors, often speaking of the times to come. The Elders had dreamed often of a massive tidal wave devastating Australia, and the prophecy still held sway in the Aboriginal communities. This was also the reason so many Elders had returned to the "country," as his father put it, to prepare their spirits and connect back to the land, back to their ancestral homes, and back where they belonged. They had seen the signs of the End of Days.

"Our people have owned this land for more than a hundred thousand years, Noah," his father said. "The land is us, and we are the land. It is our heritage and responsibility. We must protect and keep it."

"I understand."

"I know you understand. But you don't live it, son."

"Pa, the prophecy of the End of Days is only a myth. The Elders said giant earthquakes and a massive tidal wave would end the world years ago. We're still here. It's a fairy tale."

"It's our tradition. Don't dismiss it, son."

Noah shook his head.

* * *

Global unrest had intensified as Noah entered his late teenage years. Technological espionage had escalated between China, Russia, and the United States. The North Koreans continued to test nuclear arms, threatening to decimate South Korea, Japan, and even Australia. Drones the size of hornets could now carry biological payloads designed to wipe out entire cities. The Tehran Accord of 2032, intended to end nuclear proliferation in the Middle East, was, like many treaties, disregarded mere days after its signing. Civil unrest ruled every corner of the planet.

The fuse was short.

The world as Noah had known it had always been this way. Australia had largely avoided the planet's human ills. Yet, the threat of a nuclear attack from North Korea or another hostile nation on the brink always rested uneasily on his mind. For that reason, he enlisted in the military.

Noah joined the Australian Defence Force when he was seventeen, the earliest he could, hoping eventually to deploy on operations with the Army. But he knew he'd run off to the ADF to escape his home situation—which, in hindsight, his home was not as horrible as he'd thought. He later understood that it's tough to shed the blinders. He'd soon realized and came to appreciate how much his parents had sacrificed for him.

Joining the ADF provided the opportunity to move to Canberra, a modern city so different from the homestead. He'd hoped to enter the academy, but they discovered in a medical physical he had a slight arrhythmia. He could not then apply and was unable to work his way into becoming an officer. They only permitted him to become a reservist, far from his dream. He resigned from the military and got a job as a carpenter, working for a company that primarily produced doors. Not exactly the future he'd envisioned.

When his mother told him that his father was gravely ill, Noah decided there was no future for him in Canberra. His family needed him to return to the homestead, back to his people.

Soon after Noah returned, his father died suddenly of acute myocardial infarction. His mother's grief overwhelmed her, but Noah couldn't understand why she blamed the old man on the porch for his father's death.

"Your father is gone," his mother said, "yet this thing is still here, as always. It's not fair. Why should that thing live yet your father dies?" Tears sprang to her eyes. "I hate it."

"I know."

"Hate it, do you understand?"

"Yes."

"We need to kill it."

Noah looked at her for a moment, surprised. His mother would harm no one or any living thing.

"We need to kill it," she repeated.

"I don't think we can, Ma."

"If it breathes, it can die."

"How do you know it breathes?"

She didn't respond. Just stared at the old man and shook her head.

"Ma?"

"It doesn't deserve to live. It just doesn't," she whispered.

The next day, Noah found his mother dead in the road's dust in front of their home, her body stretched beneath the blistering sun, facing the sky with open eyes. She lay only fifty feet from the man's porch.

The coroner later claimed she died of a massive coronary and didn't feel a thing. Noah doubted that. She had his father's rifle in her hands when he found her. He'd removed the rifle before the authorities arrived to take her away. But he knew why she had it, what she'd attempted to do. There was a spent shell in the weapon. She'd got off one shot before she died.

The old man rocked on the porch, seeming oblivious. But Noah knew better.

Noah approached the man soon after his mother's funeral. He stood directly in front of the old man, fists clenched, yet he was stoked with fear. The man sat tall in his chair, unmoved.

"You did this," Noah said. "I know you killed her. Didn't you?"

The man said nothing.

"Did you kill my father, too? It was no heart attack, was it? You. I know it was you. How did you make him so ill? He was a strong, healthy man. I know you had something to do with this. Bastard!"

The man said nothing.

"Are you going to kill me, too? Is that your plan?"

The man said nothing. But he smiled.

Soon after, Noah built a twelve-foot fence around the old man's house, surrounding the property, cutting off the man's view of the world. Two days after he'd completed the fence, it disappeared in the night, vanished, perhaps dissolved into the atmosphere.

Noah never built another fence.

* * *

In the years to come, Noah abandoned sheep herding and redeveloped the land as an airfield, a small airport with a runway perfect for his Cessna and other light aircraft. The other nearby homesteaders relied on his services to provide food and supplies for families in secluded areas of the outback. He often wondered why Aboriginal people remained on land so inhospitable to humans, and those thoughts always drove him to remember his father and how he embraced their heritage. The lifestyle still felt so foreign to Noah.

Several times, the Australian government closed his airport as North Korea yet again threatened nuclear strikes, and the government restricted airspace. Whenever flights were banned for any length of time, his business suffered, as did the families he served. And Noah couldn't understand how limiting commercial flights helped the government protect them from missile strikes. It made no sense to him. But the air force commanded the Australian sky, and Noah could only wait until they lifted the bans to resume his business.

* * *

First, the television reception went out, which happened frequently in the outback. Not interested in most TV programming, Noah had taken to pleasure reading. He often disappeared into the worlds of Arthur C. Clarke, Robert Heinlein, Isaac Asimov, Frank Herbert, and other classic science fiction writers—worlds so different from the one in which he survived.

But this time, when he turned on the television for the weather report, something seemed … off. The screen was blank. Not just blank, but black like an abyss. No broken, wavering lines. No light at all. At first, Noah thought perhaps the TV was malfunctioning. But then he heard the voices, thousands of languages and dialects, all speaking at once, blending into an incomprehensible cacophony from hell. All the voices sounded frantic. Wailing and screams sprang to his ears like knives.

He switched off the TV. *What the hell?*

Then he noticed an odd pulsing in the sky outside his living room window.

Noah stepped through his front door and looked at the clouds. They were swirling maroon and scarlet and black and purple, swirling faster as he watched.

He turned to look at the old man on the porch. The man's head was now upturned to the angry blood sky. Noah could see he was smiling.

A global rumbling came, the thunder of the atmosphere collapsing on the other side of the world. The old man stopped rocking, apparently keen on listening to the Earth's final groan. An ominous glow emanated far to the east, the approaching conflagration devouring everything in its path. There was also a glow to the west, also encroaching.

The two approaching nuclear storms would likely meet exactly where Noah stood. Exactly where the old man had waited so long. And then Noah understood. The Elders had been right, but they only misjudged the timing. And it wasn't a massive tidal wave from an angry sea. No, it was a rolling wave of flame.

Noah watched as the old man slowly stood. He'd never seen the man leave the chair, never seen him stand. The thing—yes, the thing, Noah fully realized—stood far taller than Noah had expected, far taller than any man he'd ever known. The thing turned to Noah, smiling. Its monstrous grin contained an impossible number of teeth. He winked at Noah and then turned his face again to the reddening sky with outstretched arms. His multi-hinged jaw dropped and widened.

A scorching wind blasted across the desert from the east, its sister to the west. Noah could now see the approaching walls of flame. Massive white funnels spiraled from the sky as if pursued by the nuclear fire. The funnels contained millions of ephemeral entities, the wisps of things once human, and the funnels twisted into the enormous maw of the thing on the porch.

Noah then knew who the old man was.

The Great Consumer of Souls had waited so long for his banquet to begin.

Today, he would finally feast.

Noah waited to burn.

He did not have long to wait.

A DAY AT THE BEACH WITH THE GRAMTHROTTLEMAX FAMILY

BernluluGruk GramthrottleMax knew Rehoboth wasn't a nude beach. But he also knew that humans wouldn't know if he was naked or not. They had no clue concerning his genitalia—not knowing that his "junk," as the humans say, was safely tucked in the folds of his upper abdomen.

As soon as he and his family slithered from the ocean to get some sun on the beach, the humans scattered, screaming, snatching up their towels and children, falling over one another toward the boardwalk. They left their umbrellas, boogie boards, beach blankets, and coolers of food and drink, fearing for their lives.

At least the two GramthrottleMax kids would have plenty to play with!

The Rehoboth Beach Boardwalk fascinated GramthrottleMax. He always wanted to try the saltwater taffy at the Candy Kitchen. He heard the mint sticks were to die for. But, if he attempted to climb on the boardwalk with his massive, sluglike bulk, he surely *would* die.

And Thrasher's French Fries! He never understood why they were French—but, oh my God, he would die for those!

His mate, FrizzlegumMash, had for years hounded him to lose weight. He could certainly stand to lose a few hundred pounds. But, weighing in at three tons, he didn't see the sense of it. A bucket of fries wouldn't kill him.

"Where are the kids?' he asked.

"Oh, they've nearly finished eating the lifeguard," FrizzlegumMash said. "They were getting a bit peckish and cranky. I told them to run off and get a bite."

The two little guys, FlemrashKrup and SnoopraraNuf, were a rambunctious and ravenous pair. Of course, "little" was open to interpretation. Flem weighed a healthy half ton, and his older brother Snoop was now almost a ton. They grow so fast!

Frizzle, however, thought their offspring were undernourished. GramthrottleMax wished she thought *he* was undernourished. You can't eat kelp and plankton forever. This vegan thing was ridiculous. He managed to sneak a harbor seal, sea turtle, or scuba diver when she wasn't looking. (Although the rubber casing of the latter inevitably snarled his mandibles.)

"Bernie, did you remember to bring the suntan lotion?" she said.

"You know I can't wear that stuff. Slides right off with the rest of the slime."

"Well, don't complain of sunburn later then. But we do need to slather the kids." She turned. "Flem. Snoop. Get over here!"

GramthrottleMax loved Rehoboth Beach. Sure, he and the family often visited Atlantic City at the Jersey shore. The pollution there was delightful, and the occasional corpse floating south from New York City was a special treat (if you spit out the bullets). Ocean City, Maryland, and Virginia Beach had been frequent vacation spots, and they even traveled as far south as the Outer Banks. But his family preferred Rehoboth Beach. Unfortunately, the denizens of the Delaware beach town were not so fond of the GramthrottleMaxs. Probably that whole eating-of-humans thing.

The family usually had an hour or two on the beach until the humans started pestering them. You'd think the humans would be prepared for his family's frequent visits. But, no, it was a new adventure every time.

He reclined in the sand and sighed. A little relaxation time, even if brief, was always welcome. The life of a sea monster could be hectic, especially with a family to feed.

When he first visited Rehoboth Beach with his parents decades before, he assumed the sand would be torture. All the creases and crevices in his body, those blubbery folds and oozing orifices. GramthrottleMax thought the sand would invade every inch of his body. Which it did. But the hot beach sand effectively scraped away all the barnacles—the hotter the sand, the better. And, once back in the water, he found it easy to rinse the sand away. No problem.

His offspring had no reservations about the sand. They rolled and played, tossing sand with abandon. Flinging seashells and seagulls at each other. Making sandcastles and gleefully kicking them down. Eating the occasional human.

FrizzlegumMash, on the other hand, never really enjoyed the beach. But then she had several additional orifices that were not so sand-inviting. He understood.

GramthrottleMax knew that, apart from the sand, FrizzlegumMash would have liked nothing better than to lie back and read a good book, just like all the other beachgoers they had witnessed from the waves. Maybe something juicy, like *Shades of Gray Whale*. But, of course, publishing was next to impossible back home at the bottom of the Hatteras Abyssal Plain. So, no books. It would be difficult for her to flip through the pages anyway, having no fingers.

GramthrottleMax stared at Frizzle for a moment, admiring her elephantine nakedness. He felt lucky to have found her, and even luckier that she had accepted him. Miracles do happen. He never understood why human males get all slobbery over scrawny, stick-thin females wearing tiny string bikinis. Those females were barely snacks—no meat at all. The males get all excited over two fabric-strapped breasts. Good Lord, why? FrizzlegumMash had eight glorious breasts. What's not to love? And she was the smartest creature on the planet. Certainly smarter than he was.

"Gorgeous," GramthrottleMax said. He winked as she turned to him.

"What?" she said. "What? Do you have something in your eye?"

"No. I just wanted you to know how beautiful you are."

"I think you've been in the sun too long. Really."

"Gorgeous," he repeated.

"Bernie, how long do we have to stay here? This sand—"

"Just until the kids get tired. Or the humans decide we've worn out our welcome."

"Well, that may be sooner than you think. The humans are already being forced to leave."

GramthrottleMax turned toward the boardwalk. Many uniformed men and women were now shepherding people, orchestrating the evacuation. The usual routine, just standard human protocol. The National Guard would arrive soon. He and his family still had time to enjoy the beach before the firepower showed up.

He and Frizzle loved the mayhem that typically ensued—and the accompanying feast. He liked to think of it as a buffet on the beach. But he knew the little ones couldn't tolerate the explosions and incredibly thunderous noise for long. The screams from the humans, no problem. But the grenades and rocket launchers, not so much.

"Should we start packing?" FrizzlegumMash said.

"Nah. I think we have time. Let the kids play a little longer. Besides, I'm quite comfortable here. The sun is wonderful. The barnacles are silently screaming. And I can already feel the vitamin D building in my corpulence."

"That's nice, dear." She turned to the kids playing in the sand. "FlemrashKrup GramthrottleMax! Stop gnawing on that seagull! You'll get feathers in your mandibles!"

"Listen to your mother. We'll have enough to eat shortly. Wouldn't you much prefer a tasty human over that measly seagull?"

"Bernie! Stop it," FrizzlegumMash said, nudging him with a flipper. "You're going to spoil them."

"Aw, Mom," Flem said. He tossed the maimed seagull aside.

GramthrottleMax yawned, much like most sea monsters do. The yawn sounded simultaneously like an angry pelican and a flatulent walrus. Only sea monster vocal cords can accomplish this.

"Let me know when the soldier boys get here," he said.

He closed his eyes.

* * *

GramthrottleMax must have dozed off. How long? Maybe an hour. Maybe only minutes.

FrizzlegumMash leaned into him, waking him. "Do you hear that?"

GramthrottleMax heard them before he saw them. Fighter jets, probably scrambled from the Dover Air Force Base

No National Guard this time. Just all-out warfare. And, unfortunately, no easy meals.

The jets would arrive in seconds.

"Time to go, Frizzle," he said. "Talk about taking the fun out of it. Jets? Really? Not the National Guard? Where's the fun in that?"

There were two jets now screaming toward them from the north. At that moment, GramthrottleMax wished he'd been Godzilla, able to swat the planes from the sky. (Of course, Godzilla was an irritable bastard, and GramthrottleMax usually stayed away from him at dinner parties. That breath!)

"Flem. Snoop," he said. He heaved himself from the sand. "We need to leave now."

"Aww, Dad," they whined in unison. "Can't we stay a little longer?" Snoop said.

"We can come back another time. Perhaps next week, if the weather is nice. But, right now, you need to help your mother gather our things and head to the water."

"What things?" she said. "We're naked."

"I mean any things the kids want to take with them. Maybe a seagull or two. Your sunscreen. What's left of that lifeguard. Just hurry."

Even though the jets were still just two dots in the sky, he saw the flashes beneath them and knew missiles were on the way. He'd never dealt with missiles before, but he was always up for a new challenge.

He couldn't believe how quickly the missiles had arrived!

The first missile plunged into his gelatinous left side. GramthrottleMax immediately plucked it from his body with a tentacle and hurled it into the ocean, where it exploded in a mushroom of seawater. The wound did hurt a bit—like a bubble of gas in his intestine, something difficult to pass—but of no true concern.

He flipped the second missile into the water with his back fin. Another explosion of seawater.

The third, with a whip-like tentacle.

The fourth, slapped easily aside where it exploded in the sand.

He was getting the hang of it.

The two F-15 jets zoomed overhead. GramthrottleMax knew they would circle back for another attack.

"Get the kids into the water, Friz. As deeply and as quickly as you can. I'm their largest target, so they will pay you and the kids no mind—at least for now. Once you're safe, I'll follow."

FrizzlegumMash prodded Flem and Snoop toward the surf. But, reluctant to leave, they moved with something less than urgency, flopping more than slithering to the water. Frizzle prodded more.

"Hurry!" GramthrottleMax said. "They're returning. Get into the water!"

The jets had turned and now approached again. But he saw no flashes of missiles being deployed this time. How many missiles did the typical fighter jet carry? He had no idea. Maybe they planned a strafing run this time, which would make more sense. They didn't want to destroy the beach—just destroy him.

The jets zoomed toward him. He didn't budge, giving the pilots a massive, perfect target. He glanced over at his family. They had reached the surf and would soon find safety in the ocean.

And then the jets passed overhead. They did not attack him, for whatever reason. Maybe they'd watched him swat the earlier missiles aside and had determined that another air strike would be fruitless.

He assumed that meant the armed forces would soon arrive. That was always fun … but he'd had enough sun and fun for the day. The family was already in the water, waiting for him.

He sighed, shrugged his three shoulders, and moved toward the surf.

The GramthrottleMax family would return to Rehoboth Beach again before the summer was over. Perhaps several times.

He sure did hanker for some Thrasher's Fries!

ON THE VIADUCT

Tentacles of blue lightning slashed across the swirling, wintry sky. The snow had been coming down throughout the night, making the early Monday morning commute treacherous at best. Inches of ice sheeted the roads, and the endless snow accumulated faster than the road crews could plow it.

"Well, we're not moving," Gerald Garber said, thumping the steering wheel with his fist. The traffic on I-95 going into Wilmington was at a complete stop. His Nissan Versa was in the far-right lane on the viaduct going into the city—nowhere to turn, no way to avoid the traffic snarl. They were four hundred yards from the Delaware Avenue exit, their exit—might as well be a thousand miles away. Gerald could see flashing lights ahead, suggesting an accident scene caused by the icy road conditions. He turned to his carpool passenger, Dan Horner, with a look of exasperation.

"Figures Nate would call us into the office during the worst blizzard in Delaware history," Dan said.

"He's been trying to schedule this conference call with AstroTec Systems for weeks. This could be a multimillion-dollar account," Gerald said. "The client is based in San Antonio. They don't care if the weather sucks here."

"Still." Dan looked out the car window and shook his head. "That rat bastard Nate could manage the call himself. From his home, no less. That's probably what he's doing right now."

Gerald nodded. "Probably. But he needs us there for the numbers. Nate doesn't know jack about the financial figures. Well, if the governor had called a state of emergency and shut down the highways, we wouldn't be stuck here. Nate couldn't force us to break the law, to drive when it was illegal to be on the roads."

"Makes no sense to me," Dan said. "All the government offices and schools are closed, so why not businesses? Is Molly home with the boys?"

"Yep. Her company called and told her not to come in, so she's home with Billy and Carl."

A broad spear of sharp blue lightning split the sky, followed by a deafening *BOOM* that shook the car.

"The lightning is right overhead," Gerald said.

"That wasn't lightning. Didn't you feel that? Something crashed behind us. The whole highway shook."

"It was just thunder." But Gerald looked into the rearview mirror and saw a brief burst of azure light on the road far behind the car, a glow that at first pulsed, and then dissipated and disappeared.

"What? What'd you see?" Dan asked.

"Nothing. Maybe the lightning struck a transformer."

Dan shook his head. "I'm telling you, that wasn't lightning."

The viaduct then shuddered, followed by a rumbling to the south, like a massive train. Gerald had survived a tornado when he was younger, and the angry sound reminded him of that. Could there be a tornado during a blizzard? He'd never heard of such a thing, but assumed it was possible. Other people in cars around him began getting out of their vehicles. He started to open the car door to see what was going on when his cell phone screeched in the console between the seats. When he answered the phone, his frantic wife was on the line.

"You … home … gone …"

"Molly, what are you—?"

"Gerald! We …"

"Honey, the phone is breaking up. What are you saying? Where are the kids?"

"… it's here … something in the snow!"

She screamed. Then the phone went to static.

"Molly?"

Gerald quickly punched in his home number. Static raked into his ear.

"What's going on?" Dan asked.

A deafening, electronic growl came from the phone, and Gerald impulsively hurled it to the floor.

"I've heard nothing like that before," Dan said.

Gerald shook his head. "I don't know what's going on. Could the storm knock out the phone service?"

He stared at the phone, still vibrating like a living thing at his feet. He wanted to lift his foot and crush it, stomp the life out of it. But he couldn't. What if Molly tried to call him? He realized the phone was his only lifeline to his wife and kids.

He turned to Dan. "You didn't bring your phone?"

"I was running late. I left it on the kitchen table."

Dan was a single guy. Gerald figured he didn't have any local family to worry about. Still …

In his rearview mirror, Gerald now saw cars being tossed left and right like toys. A black mass loomed on the interstate behind him. Whatever the thing was, it stretched at least fifty feet above the highway. The enormous, slug-like monstrosity was slowly moving on the viaduct, its bulk draping both sides of the structure. It had hundreds, maybe thousands, of unblinking eyes and likely as many tentacles. What the hell was this thing?

Dan must have seen the same thing in the mirror.

"Oh my God," he said. He grasped at the door, trying to open it with shaking hands.

"Wait!" Gerald grabbed at his friend, too late.

Dan finally opened the door and stepped out.

"Dan, wait!"

But he was already running, falling on the ice, getting to his feet, running again. A mottled, gray-green tentacle snapped like a whip around Dan's midsection, bisecting and ripping him apart. His bottom half stumbled a few steps past his toppled upper torso and then fell as well. Gerald watched, horrified, as Dan's eyes widened, and his mouth gulped like a landed fish. Dan twitched for a few seconds and then stopped.

Gerald hunched against the steering wheel, shaking with instant fear. What the hell was happening? At first, he could not move, frozen in fear. This was a nightmare. He had to wake up. Wake. Up!

A tentacle lashed around his side-view mirror. A slimy, sickly green substance oozed from innumerable wide pores. The tentacle's underside had no cups like that of an octopus, but what appeared to be hinged, serrated ridges that ran along the arm's length.

Then the mirror snapped off and was tossed away.

Gerald fell to his right across the console. He gasped as something pulled at his coat. He thought the thing had already found him. But, no, his coat had snagged on the gearshift. He tugged the coat free and managed to slide into the passenger seat. Dan had left the door open.

The car rocked as he fell from the door to the ice-crusted pavement. Rock salt on the road dug into his palms and knees. The salt stung his eyes and the whipping, snow-filled wind stole his breath. His face close to the road's surface, he looked beneath the car. The thing's bulk was still a hundred yards away. But the long tentacles continued to toss cars and their occupants off the highway, the vehicles crashing in the city streets that ran beneath the viaduct.

He heard sirens wailing, booming thunder, and human screams.

Gerald rolled against the viaduct wall just as a tentacle whipped past him, seizing the open car door and wrenching it from its hinges, flinging it over the wall he was cowering against. There was a deafening roar, like that of an angry, injured animal.

Gerald realized he had to get off the highway. Even if the tentacles didn't find him, the monster's massive weight would crush him as it passed. He tilted his head to glance up at the wall he was pressed against. It was a concrete barrier, coated with snow, ice, and road debris. About ten feet ahead of him, there was an electrical conduit feeding a streetlight. The conduit extended over the wall and down the other side. Where to he could only guess. But at least it presented an option.

The car directly behind his lifted and twirled at the end of a tentacle, the woman behind the wheel screaming as the car somersaulted over the viaduct wall. Gerald heard the horrid crash of the vehicle below. He could then smell the odor of burning gasoline.

He rose to his hands and knees and forced himself to crawl to the conduit, flattening himself to the road whenever a tentacle snapped above his head. When he reached the conduit, he pressed himself to the base of the wall. A thick tentacle wrapped around his car and crushed it like an egg before tossing the mangled metal carcass aside.

Gerald removed his belt, looped it around the conduit pipe, refastened the buckle, and then quickly slid over the wall, gripping the belt with ice-numbed hands. A tentacle lashed past his leg as he went over the side, snatching the shoe from his left foot. The belt tightened around his fingers, nearly breaking them, as his body weight came to bear on the belt loop.

Dozens of tentacles continued to toss destroyed cars and bodies past him. He now barely felt his fingers. Why didn't he wear gloves today? He would soon lose his grip. With enormous effort, he pulled himself up enough to slip his right arm through the belt loop and put the pressure on the crook of his elbow. He could then release his hands. But how long could he tolerate this? The pain in his arm was excruciating.

The viaduct lurched and dropped a few inches. Fissures appeared in the concrete wall above him. The weight of the Lovecraftian nightmare was taking its toll on the viaduct's infrastructure. How soon would it collapse? How soon would falling concrete and the thing now above his head crush him? The thought of dying beneath tons of gelatinous flesh …

He had no time.

Gerald looked down. It was at least a fifty-foot drop to the street below, a street already cluttered with broken vehicles and bodies, the snow splashed with leaking blood and fuel. He probably wouldn't survive the fall, but he had to risk it. Countless tentacles thrashed above his head, and inevitably one would strike him. Frantic, he scanned below, weighing his few alternatives. There appeared to be none. Then he noticed a snowbank not quite beneath him, likely snow plowed and piled there earlier in the morning by the city street crew. It could be frozen solid, but it was a better choice than the ice-blanketed asphalt and pavement.

Drops of ichor oozing from the thing above rained on Gerald's head and shoulders. The stench, a swamp-like odor of something long dead, made him gag.

A tentacle slapped the concrete mere inches from his face.

He pulled his arm from the belt.

And dropped to the street below.

When Gerald smashed into the pile of snow, he felt something crunch in his upper back, just below his neck—a flash of agonizing pain, and then no sensation at all. He tried to roll to his side, off his back, and discovered he could not move his legs, his arms, or any part of his lower body. He must have damaged his spinal cord on impact, on a sharp edge of ice or something hidden in the snow. Gerald could move his head left to right, up and down, but nothing more. At least there was no pain.

He realized, despite the sirens sounding throughout the surrounding city, that no one would come to his aid for some time, if at all. He also realized he would never see his wife and children again. Were they even alive? He had to not think long about that.

Gerald could not turn his head far enough to see the monstrous thing on the viaduct, but he could hear the screams and the carnage on the interstate to the north, heading into the heart of Wilmington.

The snow was coming down harder now, swirling into his eyes and melting on his face as he looked skyward. The startling blue streaks of lightning were beautiful in the stark-white sky. He could see hundreds of blue arrows angling through the atmosphere.

Of course, they were not lightning, Gerald understood now. Not lightning at all.

The invasion had only just begun.

NANIMWÉ

The jagged rocks at the bottom of the ravine were painted with blood, dried brown under the desert sun. A shredded, stained bedroll and articles of clothing were scattered around the extinguished campfire. Fragmented human bones littered the site.

The Indian picked up a shattered piece of a femur, the bone stripped of muscle and sinew. Something had gnawed the cartilage at the joint.

Reid dismounted his horse and joined the Indian, a skilled scout he'd befriended in Dodge years before. A member of the Potowatomie tribe, the Indian proved to be an invaluable asset in Reid's crusade as they'd traversed the Great Plains. They had been on the trail together for so long, they rarely used one another's names—a nod or a glance was often all that was needed. Reid most often called him Nikan, a term for "friend" in his tribe's native language.

Reid pointed to a pile of scat nearby. The Indian nodded, understanding, and squatted next to the scat in the desert sand. He used his knife to pull the dried shit apart to examine its contents.

"Nanimwé," he said.

Reid nodded. "Coyote."

"Coyote, yes."

Reid saw many coyote tracks at the top of the ravine, but the tracks of what appeared to be a larger, solitary animal were here at the camp base. The other coyotes had not joined in the feast. Very odd.

"Not a wolf?"

The Indian shook his head. "Not mwé. Nanimwé."

Reid had no idea how Nikan could determine the difference. Shit was shit.

"How many victims?"

"Two men."

A coyote rarely attacked a human, much less two men. Unless it was rabid, a lone coyote would not enter a camp with a raging fire, particularly in a steep ravine where a quick escape would be difficult. Even a wolf would avoid such a camp, unless starving and desperate. Reid had seen plenty of game in the region, plenty of rabbits and rodents.

No, this was something different—and, unfortunately, familiar.

Nikan looked up at him.

Reid sighed. "Our job is not yet done."

* * *

Krupp killed the old woman without hesitation, with his bare hands around her throat. He probably would have raped her first if she weren't so ancient. Her even-more-ancient husband had given him more trouble, had fought back, but the man's corpse now rested in the parlor on the first floor. He dropped the woman to the bedroom floor like so much soiled laundry.

Krupp went downstairs, looked at the old man again, and smiled. He'd heard rumors the rich landowner had a stash of money and silver. When he saw the expanse of the ranch, he had no problem believing it. And when he saw the fine silverware laid out on the dining room table, he had no doubt.

He had plenty of time to find the hidden loot, but killing was such a tiring endeavor. He plopped on the davenport to rest for a moment, kicking the man's arm out of his way as he did so.

A wealthy man like this surely had a liquor cabinet somewhere in the house. Krupp hadn't tasted bourbon in a good many months, only rot-gut beer tasting like warm piss. Maybe he'd look for the liquor first. No hurry.

He fell asleep on the sofa.

* * *

The sun had disappeared behind the western range of mountains hours ago. Reid leaned against a boulder near the campfire, unable to sleep. His Indian friend lightly snored nearby, sleeping on a blanket on the other side of the fire. Reid looked to the open sky, to the incredible field of stars unadulterated by clouds. He knew all the constellations, all the moon's phases. Perhaps the night sky was now the only true constant in his life—and it was magnificent in its beauty.

He hoped to see a shooting star. Something that, strangely, always reminded him of Martha. He knew she was up there. Somewhere. Watching down on him. Maybe smiling. He hoped so.

He could never erase the memory. Nor would he want to. The memory gave his life purpose.

Martha had died in escalating agony, her breathing ragged and sporadic, her eyes squeezed shut, with blood pooling on the ground beneath her. Reid sat with her head on his lap. He gently stroked her hair with his right hand and wiped the beading sweat from her brow with his left. She shivered against him, weakly pulling him toward her.

Just a matter of time now, he'd thought. He'd tried to hold back his tears, but it proved impossible. His wife was dying.

Martha grimaced, grinding her teeth as if to block the monstrous pain.

Her eyes snapped open, looking up at him, her eyes now also brimming with tears. But then she smiled, despite the blood at the corners of her mouth.

"Thank you," she whispered.

Reid pulled her closer and kissed her pale forehead.

"I'm sorry," he said. "I wish it could have been different. I'm so sorry."

"Love … you," she said.

Her eyes then stared at nothing, and the smile faded.

She was gone.

Reid wiped the tears from his eyes with the back of his hand and kissed her on the forehead again. "Love you, too."

He closed her eyes with his fingers and lowered her to the ground.

He was so sorry it had to be this way.

That he'd taken her life. It had to be.

And there it was—a shooting star gliding across the night skies. Reid smiled. He realized it was merely a rock disintegrating in the upper atmosphere, merely a blazing cinder. But what a grandiose, gorgeous ending.

He closed his eyes, thinking of Martha.

Sleep soon found him.

* * *

Krupp woke up in a jail cell, his head pounding. He remembered walking into the town, his pocket filled with silver coins. He'd even hidden some silverware and coins in his boots just in case someone searched his pockets. After many encounters with the law, he found the precautions wise.

He remembered walking into the saloon. But he couldn't remember beyond that. Did he really drink that much? He'd hoped to buy the extravagance of a whore, but that apparently didn't happen. At least he couldn't remember dropping his pants.

The smell was horrendous. A chamber pot, filled to overflowing and buzzing with flies, rested in a corner of the cell. When was the last time that thing had been emptied and cleaned? He could taste the stench in his dry mouth. He rubbed his eyes, which only intensified the pain in his head, and then raised his head.

The tall, wide-shouldered man looking through the bars wore a badge.

"Well, good mornin' there, sunshine," the burly man said.

Krupp sat on the bunk's edge, holding his throbbing head between his hands. "Where the hell am I?"

"Abaddon's Way. We hauled your ass in here, drunk."

"And who are you?"

"Marshal James Akins. But you can call me your worst nightmare."

"Drunk, huh?"

"Where'd you get all that money?"

Krupp pushed himself from the cot, touching the boots on his feet as he did so. Some silverware was still where he'd hidden it. His pockets, however, were empty.

"Seems you relieved me of that money."

"It ain't yours."

"Nor yours. If you think I'm a thief, you're even more so."

"I'm the law here."

"That what you call it?"

Akins tapped the bars with a rough knuckle. He grinned, revealing brown teeth. "You're not fully aware of your situation."

"I got a hangover and I'm sitting in a shitty jail. That's my situation."

"Get up."

"What?"

"Get up. It's time for you to go."

Akins opened the cell door, swung it open.

Krupp slowly stood, barely maintaining his balance. His stomach gurgled mercilessly. When was the last time he'd eaten?

"Come on, come on. I ain't got all day," Akins said.

"I ain't in no hurry."

Akins suddenly grabbed Krupp by the right shoulder, spun him around, punched him in the neck, and sent him sprawling to the floor. He hauled the man to his feet and shoved him out of the cell, and then out the jailhouse door to the street.

"You ain't gotta be rough about it," Krupp said through clenched teeth.

"We don't want or need your kind 'round here."

"My kind?" Krupp said. "What's my kind?"

Akins spat in the dirt at the man's feet. "Filthy drifter. Parasite. Scavenger. Thief. Stealing … and probably killin'."

"I never killed nobody."

"Maybe not, as scrawny as you are. Like a farm rat. But that money came from somewhere. I don't know where you stole it, you sorry sonofabitch. I'm lettin' you off easy by takin' you to the town limits."

"Thank you so much."

"If I catch you in my town again, I'll say hello with a bullet. Understood?"

"Crystal clear, marshal. I ain't got no intention of coming back to this horseshit town. Nothin' here I want no more."

* * *

Krupp stoked the campfire with a stick, watching the sparks dance. There was something about fire that fascinated him. The fast, devouring destruction perhaps, turning everything to ash. He liked the flames.

He'd love to see Abaddon's Way reduced to ash. He'd especially love to see Marshal Akins fully ablaze. There had to be some way to have his revenge on that fool.

The can of beans was far from appetizing, and he'd grown so tired of eating beans day after day. At least he didn't need to eat them with his fingers this time. He had the fork he'd stolen and hidden in his boot. It wasn't much cleaner than his fingers and reeked of foot sweat, but it would do.

He then noticed movement in the darkness at the perimeter of his camp. Red eyes surrounded him, and he knew immediately they were coyotes. Probably at least a dozen of them, prowling back and forth, frightened of the campfire. He picked up a nearby rock and hurled it at them, hitting one and hearing the resulting yelp.

"Get the hell outta here, you stinkin' bastards!"

Most of them backed away, but one did not. It moved forward, apparently unafraid. The coyote had luminous blue eyes, far brighter than the others. Funny, he'd never seen that before. And the coyote looked bigger than the others. The pack leader, maybe? Something about this frightened him as the coyote moved closer.

The thing then stood erect on two legs, its body covered with coarse hair and the head elongated like a coyote's. But Krupp knew it wasn't a coyote—perhaps part coyote, but far more. The eyes were not canine, but human. There was intelligence behind the eyes, but also hunger. Krupp was most puzzled by the pair of full breasts—clearly human breasts—that swelled from the creature's chest.

He reached for his gun just as the thing lunged at him. The first shot went high, but the second struck the thing's right shoulder, spinning it in the air before it dropped into the dust. The creature quickly rolled over and sprang to its haunches, ready to pounce again, when Krupp pumped the trigger four times, slamming four more slugs into the monster's chest. It lurched, four massive, bloody holes in those incredible breasts—but the thing still did not fall. It laughed, a distinctive female laugh. Shrill, defiant. Then it jumped again.

Krupp threw his empty gun at its head, immediately realizing how stupid that was. The creature drove him to the ground, on his back. He tried to hold the thing away from him, its teeth snapping above his face, showering him with foul-smelling drool. She was too strong for him. And then the creature sank its teeth into his left shoulder, sinking to the bone, and Krupp screamed in utter agony. The thing shook its head, trying to get a better purchase on his flesh, and began tugging at the shoulder, tearing skin and muscle.

Krupp felt around for a rock, a branch, anything to strike the monster. His hand fell on the fork, still in the can of beans. When the creature lifted its head, he plunged the fork into its right eye.

The thing fell away from him, grasping at the fork buried in its eye. The creature howled in pain, unable to yank the fork from its face. It fell to the ground, writhing and flailing its arms and legs. And then Krupp heard the strangest thing. The creature cried. He could see tears streaming from its undamaged eye. Then came wracking sobs, far too human sobs. And then the thing stopped moving.

Stranger still, the creature shrank, curling into a fetal position, and the hair gradually retracted into the skin, revealing a teenage girl. A filthy, dead, naked teenage girl with a fork protruding from her eye.

Krupp stood and slowly approached her. He poked her with his boot. She was dead alright. But what was she? He'd seen nothing like this. Nor did he ever want to see it again.

Then he realized his left shoulder was no longer painful. He rubbed it with his right hand. Although there was blood on his torn shirt, there was no wound, no ripped flesh. The damaged shoulder had healed in mere minutes. How could that happen? Nothing that had occurred in the past ten minutes made sense.

And then he realized just how hungry he was.

* * *

An extinguished campfire, still with glowing embers at the base, had been pitched near a stand of mesquite. The fire was built the night before and whoever had built it was not far gone. An empty can of beans, now crawling with ants, had been tossed aside.

The dead girl, naked and filthy, was spread on the sand on her stomach, her head twisted toward them. *She was no doubt attractive once*, Reid thought. What was most bizarre was the fork protruding from her right eye socket.

"How many?" Reid asked.

The Indian scanned the ground, walking around the camp and looking at the tracks. "One man," he said. "There is blood here, on this side of the camp. Not the girl. Must be the man."

Reid also studied the scene. "I don't see the girl's footprints. Her feet are bare. There are only animal tracks."

"One animal here," Nikan said. "Nanimwé."

"The fork. Is it silver?"

The Indian yanked the fork from her eye, examined it, and nodded. "Sanyasuk, yes."

Silver, of course. That explained everything.

Reid dismounted his horse and approached the corpse. She was a teenager. Maybe eighteen or nineteen. Just a child.

He sighed and looked toward his Indian friend.

"She the nanimwé?" Nikan said.

Reid nodded. "I think so, yes. But who killed her?"

"Man was here."

"A man here alone. That's unusual. Few solitary travelers in this area. Are you able to track him?"

Nikan walked around the area again, eyes to the ground. He shook his head.

"Maybe. But tracks not strong. Not a heavy man."

"Well, we need to go as far as we can."

Reid knew whoever killed this girl was likely now nanimwé himself.

* * *

Krupp always heard a full moon can change a man into an animal. At least, that was the legend. He thought most legends were crocks, but current affairs had shifted his thinking. He knew now, however, the tale was only partially true. He could transform at will. But it took less effort when the moon, full or not, hung in the night sky.

He wished the damnable coyotes would stop following him though, as if he were one of them, one of their pack.

His first transformation only three nights before had been unexpected and horrendously excruciating. When he'd dropped to all fours and watched the canine hair bristling on his arms and legs, felt his face stretching into a snout and his teeth enlarging in their bloodied gums, he immediately thought of the girl. The bitch had bitten him! So, that part of the legend was true—you get bitten by a werecritter, you become a werecritter.

The odd thing was, he didn't think of it as a curse at all. It offered him freedom as he'd never known before. Now he feared nothing. When he met those three cowhands on the trail the previous night, he was already hungry. He'd already become the creature, the werecoyote. He ripped the men apart and ate their hearts first. Then their livers. He ate until he was satiated, and never felt so strong and alive.

He turned back toward Abaddon's Way. He had a score to settle.

* * *

When Krupp reentered the town, he went to the saloon, knowing the barkeep would likely remember him.

He sat at the bar. "I'll have a whiskey straight up," he said.

"I don't think so," the barkeep said.

Krupp slapped a five-dollar gold coin on the counter. The cowhands had carried a good amount of money in their pockets, and he'd relished the opportunity to steal it from them. They'd no longer need it, after all. "This should be more than enough to cover it."

"Your money ain't welcome here."

"Don't you mean *I* ain't welcome here? 'Cause I'm sure your sorry ass would never turn down cash."

The man pulled a shotgun from beneath the counter and held the end of the barrel mere inches from Krupp's face.

Krupp smiled.

"You find this funny?" the barkeep said.

"I think it's pathetic."

Krupp had already begun his transformation when the man had lifted the gun. He quickly twisted and ripped the gun from the man's hands before he could pull the trigger, snapping the man's wrist. The barkeep screamed as Krupp's right hand, claws extended, raked across the man's throat, carving the larynx from his neck, and dropping the lump of flesh on the counter. The man grabbed at his throat, now pulsing gouts of blood, before dropping to the floor.

As Krupp turned toward them, his snout extending and muscles bulging, the half-dozen men seated in the saloon cleared out in less than a minute, scrambling for the door. Except for one man who stood slowly at his table, pulling his gun as Krupp faced him.

"Stand away from the bar," the man said.

Krupp continued to change as he dropped to all fours.

"What the hell are you?" the man said, his gun not wavering.

Krupp recognized the badge on the man's chest. Probably Akins's deputy.

He reared up on his hind legs and charged toward the man.

The deputy fired three shots, striking Krupp in the chest and hurling him to the floor.

Then Krupp jumped to his feet, the bloodless bullet holes already closing and disappearing.

He chuckled.

"What the ..." the deputy said, just before Krupp tore off his head.

* * *

Reid cleaned his six-shooters, polishing them as if they were gold, as if they were his children. They'd saved him more than once and would likely save him again. His number of bullets was dwindling, however. He'd have to go home soon to replenish his supply.

When Nikan had found the clean stream, they'd stopped so they and their horses could drink, and they could refill their canteens. There was also a small patch of red yucca the horses could feast on, their first food in two days.

He and Nikan had discovered three slain men—what was left of them—the day before. The nanimwé was at least a day ahead of them on the trail. Nikan could now follow the man's tracks, heading southwest.

"He's headed to Abaddon's Way," Reid said.

"He probably already there," Nikan said.

"That's what I fear. We need to be prepared, my friend."

Reid closed his eyes. He hated it when a nanimwé entered a town. The death toll was always high. Violence was always inevitable.

* * *

Krupp hadn't killed Marshal Akins as he'd planned. Instead, he decided to become the ruler, the king, of Abaddon's Way, using fear to enslave the townsfolk. Akins was helpless to stop him. Surely, to the marshal, that was more torturous than death.

Krupp stood before the man in the jailhouse, backing him into one cell. At first, Akins pulled his gun. But, as Krupp became the creature, the marshal dropped the gun and backed away.

"Still think I'm a filthy drifter? A parasite? What did you call me, a scrawny farm rat? I could strip your face off your skull and feed it to you. Want to feast on your own face?"

"What are you?" Akins said.

"You can call me your worst nightmare. Remember sayin' that to me, Akins?" Krupp smiled. "Get in the damn cell. The same one you had me in. I see you still haven't emptied the pot. I think you'll regret that."

"For God's sake, what do you want?"

"Nothin' you can offer. You just get the pleasure of watchin' me take over your precious town. Maybe even watch me eat one or two of your lovely, delicious citizens."

Krupp shut and locked the cell door. Akin sat on the stained cot, looking at the floor. "God help us all," he whispered.

* * *

Jake Springer took considerable pride in being the fastest, most accurate gunslinger in the region. Some folks considered him a vigilante. Not quite. He had never unholstered his guns without payment. Truth was, he was a hired killer. He'd lucked out when he came to Abaddon's Way. The townsfolk offered him a sack of money, more than he'd seen in some time, to kill a "monster." He'd met and shot a good many nasty men, but he never thought of them as monsters. Some were bigger than others, and some were smarter than others, but, in the end, they were all just men. And when he saw the puny man on the street … this was the monster? The man wasn't even armed.

"Hey, you!" he yelled.

The man turned toward Springer. And, as he did so, began to change. Springer then became more apprehensive. What was this? The small man's muscles bulged, a thick mat of hair formed on his arms, and his face became a long canine snout. The thing's teeth enlarged within its gaping mouth.

"You mean me?" the creature said.

Damned if that thing don't look like a coyote, Springer thought.

He pulled his pearl-handled guns and fired once from each, both bullets hitting the thing's forehead dead-on. The creature staggered but didn't go down.

What the hell?

The creature laughed, reached into a nostril, and yanked out a lead slug like a bloody nugget of snot, and then tossed it to the ground. The thing did the same with the other nostril. Two spent bullets in the dust.

Springer turned to run, something he'd never done in his life. But the monster tackled him before he'd traveled more than a few yards. The thing drove him to the ground on his face, flipped him on his back, plunged its clawed fists through Springer's rib cage, and then ripped out his still-beating heart.

Just before he died, Springer realized the townspeople hadn't paid him enough.

* * *

Reid and Nikan reached Abaddon's Way around midday, the sun blazing in the sky and baking everything beneath it. The streets were vacant, although Reid saw many frightened faces hiding behind window curtains and behind slightly open doors. The first clues the nanimwé was in town.

Nikan stopped at the center of the street. He pointed to a pool of dried blood in the dust. Someone had suffered a horrible death here.

Yet another clue.

"Where is he?" Reid said.

Nikan shrugged. "Anywhere."

They sauntered through the center of town, fully vigilant. The creature could indeed be anywhere.

Then the nanimwé, already in its full creature form, strutted out of the saloon in front of them. It stopped at the center of the street and turned toward them. The nanimwé cocked its head, seeming inquisitive.

Reid reached to his belt and unclasped his holster. He placed his hand on the handle of his weapon.

"What's this, another hired gun?" Krupp laughed.

Reid didn't respond. He merely pulled his revolver from its holster. He twirled it in his skilled hand and pointed it toward the werecoyote. This was one of the smallest ones he'd seen, but still just as deadly. The thing could rip out his throat if it got close enough. He would ensure it never did.

"What, not wantin' to talk to me?" Krupp said. He smiled.

Reid knew talking was a waste of time. There was nothing to say to this creature. Nothing could change the situation or change the confrontation's outcome.

The thing growled and shook its head, throwing foamed saliva from a mouth bristling with teeth. Then it attacked.

Reid fired once, only once.

The bullet slammed into Krupp's chest just above the left nipple. Blood spouted and blossomed like a rose in the bright sunlight.

"Impossible," Krupp said, reaching for the gushing wound. He swayed, astonishment on his face, and then toppled face-first onto the street.

After a silent moment, the Indian stepped forward and prodded the coyoteman's head with his foot. The man no longer looked canine, no longer nanimwé, but like the filthy drifter he was.

Nikan looked at his friend. "Dead."

Reid holstered his revolver and stepped toward the corpse. "Good always triumphs over evil, old friend," he said. "Perhaps he's the last of his kind."

"Doubt it."

"I doubt it, too."

Reid looked at the townsfolk hesitantly coming toward them, their eyes on the corpse, as if expecting the thing to rise from the dead.

"Yes," Reid said, turning away from the crowd. "We ride on."

* * *

A crowd surrounded Krupp's body in the middle of the street. An older man, the town's undertaker, reached down and took the man's wrist. No pulse. The thing was truly and finally dead.

The undertaker turned his head and watched the backs of the Texas Ranger on his large white horse and the Indian on his spotted palomino as they left Abaddon's Way. He scratched his chin, wondering. But it couldn't be.

They were only a legend.

THE LAST HOOKY

Mr. McCardy, the truant officer, lurked in every shadow, ready to snare any errant student. Yet, Tommy Makepeace had eluded his grasp since the beginning of the school year. Tommy knew his luck was running thin, so he planned one last day of hooky to go swimming at Silver Lake. Indian summer had arrived, and he knew the bitter weather was only a week or so away.

He caught up with Joey Cranston in the school hallway the day before. "Joey, let's play hooky," Tommy whispered in his ear. "Just one last hooky, down by the lake. Whaddaya say?"

Joey shook his head, as he always did when the topic of skipping school arose. "My father would whip the tar outta me."

"Oh, c'mon! This might be our last chance."

"Can't. Sorry."

"Sissy!"

So, Tommy decided to go solo.

* * *

Tommy hated his parents. They'd decided, without soliciting his opinion, to pack up and move to another town several hundred miles away. He thought that would land him somewhere near the heart of darkest Africa. It didn't. His worst fears unrealized, he was relieved and perhaps a bit disappointed to find that Middletown, Delaware, was a town identical to the one he'd just left in Virginia.

There was one horrible difference. In Middletown, Tommy was the strange kid, the outsider not yet accepted. Joey Cranston latched on to him like a puppy and that stupid Susan Sullivan kept trying to talk to him in the cafeteria and on the playground—but they didn't count. He had no friends. That's why Tommy played hooky.

The only fun aspect of moving to Middletown was the Everett Theater. His father was the projectionist, so Tommy sat in the projection booth every Friday night to watch the newly released movies and double features. He loved *Abbott & Costello Meet Frankenstein*, *Abbott & Costello Meet the Killer*, *Mighty Joe Young*, *Angel and the Bad Man* and other John Wayne westerns, and especially the serials, like "Batman and Robin" and "Flash Gordon." He loved watching movies with his father.

Maybe he didn't hate his parents after all.

* * *

As Tommy raced down Hoffecker Street toward the east side of town, Mr. McCardy suddenly turned the corner at the end of the block ahead of him. Tommy dove behind the huge hydrangea in front of old lady Tyler's house. He hunkered down, praying that the truant officer hadn't seen him. Large black boots stopped on the sidewalk not three feet in front of him. The massive boots reminded him of the Frankenstein monster's. He held his breath. From under the bush, he heard McCardy mutter, "Damn kids." Then the man moved on down the block.

Once he was sure McCardy was no longer nearby, Tommy ran the rest of the way to the edge of town. From Farmer Green's fields, he could reach the forest that surrounded Silver Lake by working his way through the millions of rows of dry field corn. A twelve-year-old boy could find plenty of places to hide out there.

Tommy loved Indian summer. The days were still warm but getting shorter. The leaves made their magnificent metamorphosis, creating splashes of fiery orange and red throughout the trees. Who needs musty books and cold desks and cranky teachers screeching chalk on blackboards? The forest taught him more in a day than a legion of teachers could in a year.

When Tommy reached the edge of the forest, he hurried to the stream that fed the lake. He took off his shoes, stuffed his socks inside, and tied the laces so that he could hang the shoes around his neck. He then waded into the stream. He overturned rocks on the bottom to watch crayfish scoot backward in tiny puffs of mud. Tommy wondered if they were really alien creatures that, if you weren't careful, would burrow into your flesh. He couldn't imagine anything worse than being infested with crayfish.

Tommy then searched for gold along the path, pretending to be Humphrey Bogart in *The Treasure of the Sierra Madre*. He often found chunks of quartz with what looked like gold speckled throughout. As he gathered rocks along the trail, he noticed a rock protruding from the ground like a miniature tombstone. Tommy tugged the stone free and wiped off the soil. The stone was perfectly flat and oval, polished smooth by time. He rubbed it between thumb and forefinger, and knew immediately what to do with it. He smiled and stuffed it into his shirt pocket with the other stones he'd collected.

When he reached Mighty Joe Oak, he knew he was nearly to the lake. Tommy named the tree because it was the biggest in the forest, maybe older than time itself. And he had seen *Mighty Joe Young*, his all-time favorite movie, at the Everett Theater with his father.

A squirrel spiraled up the trunk and disappeared into the tangle of branches above. Tommy decided to follow it. He had climbed the tree many times, but this day he went up higher than he'd ever braved before. He pretended to be Mighty Joe Young saving the little girl from the burning orphanage, hanging from a branch by one hand miles above the ground.

Tommy froze, instantly aware that someone was watching him. A faint rustling noise came from below. McCardy? Because the leaves were so dense, he could only see the forest floor directly below him. Was that a moving shadow? Or just a play of sunlight through the limbs? Probably just another squirrel.

Tommy sat perfectly still on the branch for what seemed like hours until the eerie sense of being watched had passed. He shimmied down the tree. It was time to go to the lake—no more dilly-dallying!

He wanted one last swim in Silver Lake.

He hoped Mr. McCardy wasn't waiting there to cuff him.

* * *

The lake was eerily quiet. A subtle breeze rippled its surface. Tommy walked to the edge of the water and looked down at his distorted reflection.

Something stirred behind him, near the huge willow that stretched its feathery limbs across the water.

Oh no! Tommy thought. *Not McCardy. Not now!*

As he slowly turned, he heard a giggle.

Sitting beneath the willow was Susan Sullivan.

"I thought you'd be here, Tommy Makepeace," she said. She smiled at him the way she always did. She never smiled like that at anyone else. "Where's Joey Cranston?"

"Joey's too chicken to skip school," he said. He tried not to look into her eyes. They were traps to snare his soul. "I didn't think girls played hooky."

"Most don't. I do."

His eyes met hers. For some reason, he felt that years, long years, bridged that gaze as if he'd known her forever. He had to look away, break the spell, but could not. She instead broke the gaze. He immediately wondered who was bewitching whom.

"It's nice here by the lake," she said. "I think I know why you come."

"I come 'cause I want to be alone."

"That's not true. You hate being alone. This is the only place that makes you happy." She sighed. "I've been waiting here for you for so long."

Tommy turned again to the lake. He reached into his shirt pocket and pulled out some stones.

"I like to skip stones," he said. "That's why I come out here."

"How good are you?"

"The best."

He tested a stone in his hand, then hurled it. The stone hopped twice, but then angled too steeply and plunged into the water. The next stone skipped five times. He wasn't satisfied. Joey had skipped a rock seven times and Joey was just a sissy. Besides, Susan was watching.

He pulled out the special stone, the one that reminded him of a tiny tombstone. It was all in the wrist and letting go at the precise moment, putting a perfect spin on the stone. He closed his eyes, concentrated, and then let it fly.

The stone skipped ten times!

He turned to Susan with a victorious grin.

"I could never do that," she said, returning his smile.

"That's 'cause you're a girl." *Just a stupid girl*, he thought. But he liked the way she smiled at him.

He sat under the willow beside her. They stared at the placid water. He wanted to say something to Susan, anything, but the words would not come. Maybe he didn't have to say anything.

He pulled at tufts of grass by his side. A long, thin blade happened into his fingers. He plucked it from the earth, rolled it gingerly between his fingers just to feel its wonderfully green texture, and then inserted it between his two top-front teeth. The blade of grass tasted like autumn. He could almost savor the waning sun, the slight chill in the air. He lay back on the soft grass to watch the clouds drift above the willow branches. The only sound, high in the tree, was that of a cicada, its raspy drone getting louder but oddly comforting.

Susan stretched out next to him on the grass. Her hand touched his. He didn't resist.

This is the place he always wanted to be, a forever place. He closed his eyes and smiled.

Tommy didn't see the long shadow extend across his prostrate form or McCardy's dark, massive hand reaching down for him ...

* * *

The green line on the EKG monitor flattened.

Dr. Kahlil switched off the monitor to end the drone of the EKG alarm. He then turned to Joe Cranston, who sat alone next to the hospital bed. "I'm sorry."

Cranston took Tom's hand in his own. The hand wasn't cold yet. "He had a heart as big and as strong as a horse."

"The cancer had pretty much spread throughout his lymphatic system," Dr. Kahlil said.

Tom nodded. "He called me Joey last night. Hadn't called me that since we were kids." He sighed and then shook his head. "Ever since Susan died three years ago, I guess he had nothing left. No kids. Not like they didn't try. They were childhood sweethearts. You'd think they'd invented love, they were so compatible.

"Last night, Tom was lucid for just a moment. He looked me straight in the eye and said, 'Joey, let's play hooky. Just one last hooky, down by the lake. Whaddaya say?' Before I could answer, his eyes lost their focus, and I knew he'd left me behind. He always left me behind. I guess I've always been afraid.

"Tommy always loved to play hooky."

MELVIN AND THE HAUNTED MANSION

I was ten years old the first time I saw Melvin. It would not be my last time.

My parents had taken the family to Rehoboth Beach, my first visit, back in 1972. The Rupert clan went to the beach often after that, we loved Rehoboth so much.

My father loved the Haunted Mansion, and he looked forward to taking me on the ride. "Tommy, you're going to love it. Trust me." My mother objected, of course. "He'll have nightmares," she said. My father knew better. Looking back, I think this was a rite of passage to him. Of course, I loved the dark ride and immediately wanted to do it again.

The ride only operated at night, so I was already hesitant when we first stood in line in front of the building. A vulture on the roof. A skeletal figure standing in a window on the second floor. A fully dressed corpse, arms extended, hanging from the wall above. When we got in line, I grabbed my father's hand. He looked down at me and smiled. "It'll be okay, kiddo."

I knew I was in for an awesome experience even before the car smashed through the dark red, swinging doors at the start of the ride. At the entrance, a huge white board had the words "Keep Arms & Legs Inside Car At All Times," with a severed zombie arm displayed above it. Was there something in there that could snap off your arms and legs if you didn't heed the warning? What monsters would I see? Vampires? Things with tentacles? Worse?

Of course, what I saw was far from ominous. We went through the Graveyard, with a large tombstone that read "YOU." The Ice Caves, filled with enormous bats and a miner threatening to blow us up with dynamite. A cool 3-D Skull Room, with dancing skulls surrounded by mirrors. And undoubtedly the best scene was the Living Room, with an open coffin and a creepy ghoul playing a pipe organ. The Mansion was filled with secret passages, plenty of skeletons, and even a Frankenstein monster. I felt scared, but it was a fun scare; my father was laughing with me throughout the ride. I loved it!

Looking back now, after all the decades, the Haunted Mansion on the Rehoboth boardwalk paled in comparison to the Mansion in Mouse Town in Orlando. But that attraction is way too slick, too commercial, and far too wrapped up in its own technical aspects. Far too sanitized for my taste. The dark ride on the boardwalk had a carny feel to it—which is not a bad thing at all, I think. Sure, it may be cheesy, but that's the charm of the place. To this day, I visit the attraction every chance I get.

But I'm getting ahead of myself. This is about Melvin.

The first time I rode the ride was the first that I saw Melvin. He was the ride attendant, taking our tickets and ushering us into the car suspended from an overhead track. I knew his name was Melvin because I saw it embroidered on his shirt pocket, with red lettering on a white background and a dark red border. No last name. Just MELVIN.

And Melvin was creepy as hell! He was bald and had huge ears that were disproportionate to his face. Pig-like nose, broad with wide nostrils. His eyes were misaligned—one eye skewed to the left, while the other eye was directed toward the ceiling. When we approached him with our tickets, my father said, "Hi! How ya doing?" Melvin didn't respond, didn't even acknowledge our presence. When our car pulled up beside us, Melvin stepped forward to raise the bar and we seated ourselves. He lowered the bar and stepped back. And the ride began.

"He's just acting," my father said, "pretending to be a zombie."

But I wasn't so sure.

* * *

The Haunted Mansion was a favorite beach attraction for horny teenage couples looking to cop a feel. You could get to second base if you were fast enough—the ride wasn't that long.

When I was sixteen, I managed to talk Norma Johnson into going on the ride with me. Super shy and super gorgeous, she resisted going on the ride at first. But then I pointed out all the children in the line— "C'mon, they're little kids"—and she gave in.

I hadn't visited the boardwalk for the past three years. The man taking our tickets was someone I'd not seen before. He looked bored to tears.

"Is Melvin still around?" I asked.

The guy looked at me like I had a venereal disease. "Don't know any Melvin," he said.

I assumed Melvin had retired or moved on. Who could afford to stay at this job for years? Who knows, maybe he died.

As the ride began and we entered the darkness, Norma was quiet and clearly uncomfortable. I pulled her close and put my arm around her shoulders.

"Nothing to worry about," I said. "Just remember, it's all for fun."

She nodded but didn't say anything. She shivered.

"Never been through a haunted house before, huh?"

"Never," she said. "And I wouldn't be doing it now if I didn't like you so much, Tommy."

She loosened up when we went past the Graveyard display—with the tombstone engraved with "Here Lies Jake—Hit the Gas Instead of the Brake."

"Well, that's just silly," she said, and smiled at me. That smile made my heart melt.

We kissed for the first time as the car went past the 3-D Skull Room. I slipped my left hand under her right breast as we arrived at the Living Room—and then I saw Melvin standing next to the ghoulish organist. He wore totally black attire, and I might have missed him standing there if I hadn't been paying attention. He seemed to blend into the scene, seemed to be a part of the display. Melvin didn't look directly at us as we went slowly by, but his head turned as the car moved through the room. I thought it odd to see him there, so many years later, and I suddenly felt ill at ease. Something seemed wrong. I pulled my hand away from Norma. And then our car turned a corner and Melvin was no longer in my line of vision.

"Did you see that?" I asked.

"What?"

"The man back there?"

She shook her head. "I didn't see anything."

And then she gently pulled my hand back to her chest.

* * *

I went off to Clemson University, down in South Carolina, in 1981, pursuing a degree in graphic design. I lived in Greenville for those four years and visited Myrtle Beach a few times during the summers. But Myrtle Beach didn't have the flavor or charm of Rehoboth, and I yearned for my home beach—and to return to the Haunted Mansion. But I didn't return to Delaware until 1986, and, because of job circumstances, didn't get back to the boardwalk until late in the summer of '87.

For the next few years, I went to Rehoboth several times each summer, with family or friends. Went to the Mansion each time. I did not see Melvin and was strangely disappointed. I wanted so much to see him there. He was part of my memory of Rehoboth.

* * *

In 1990, I married my beautiful wife, Diane. We had our first child, Ben, in 1991. With a newborn and now a shared life, we had little opportunity for vacation time. I worked a fifty-hour week at a publisher in Philadelphia. The commute alone was hellacious, particularly when I-95 was choked with traffic. But in the summer of '93, Diane convinced me that we needed some time off. So, we went to Rehoboth for a few days of fun and relaxation. By that time, Ben was a toddler and could handle some of the kiddie rides in Funland. So, one night we went to the boardwalk. As we went from ride to ride, from the Kiddy Wheel to the Carousel, I kept glancing over toward the Mansion only a short distance away, and Diane caught me.

"Go ahead," she said. "I know you're dying to."

"You sure?"

"Sure. Ben is having too much fun and probably won't even notice you're gone. I'll take him on the merry-go-round."

I smiled and nodded. "OK, I'll be right back."

As I stood in line for the ride, I realized the attraction needed love. The facade could use a fresh coat of paint. As I started the ride, I noticed several of the gimmicks no longer worked. Of course, most folks wouldn't notice. But I remembered, I'd been on the ride so many times over the years. I knew every room, every monster, every ghoul.

The car then entered the mirrored room with the floating skulls. The glowing skulls danced on their wires, moving up and down as they always did.

Melvin stood at the back of the room in the shadows, briefly illuminated by the dim lights above the mirrors. I saw his bald head, the eyes askance and unfocused, looking exactly like the zombie I remembered. As I went through the small room, I could see his reflection in the mirrors at different angles. He did not move, did not watch my car slowly pass by. He remained frozen in place, blending into the scene.

As the car moved around a corner toward the next room, I turned in the seat to look back. One second, he was there. The next, gone.

How could it be possible? It made no sense. How could a man I first saw at the Haunted Mansion back in 1972 still be here in 1993? Even back then, he looked to be in his late forties, maybe older. He would have been in his sixties by now. If he was still alive.

I don't remember getting off the ride after that. I made my way through Funland and found Diane standing next to the Fire Truck ride, watching Ben travel in lazy circles, turning the steering wheel with such enthusiasm that he probably thought he controlled the truck. She turned to me with a smile, but quickly realized something was wrong.

"What?" she asked.

"I don't know. I think I just saw a ghost."

"Well, sure. It's a haunted house."

"No, I mean it. I think I saw a *ghost*."

Diane looked at me as if I'd just grown a third arm.

"I'm serious," I said. "I saw a man in there, the same man I saw on this ride when I was ten."

"Maybe he works here."

"No, I don't think so. He would be so old now. He just stood there, in the shadows. And it's not the first time I've seen him in the Mansion."

"Maybe you're mistaken. Probably just a dummy, a prop, just part of the ride. And you thought you saw this guy. A trick of the imagination."

"Maybe," I said. I looked back at the Mansion. "But I don't think so."

* * *

My father gradually slipped into dementia when he was seventy. Mom had died of lung cancer a decade before, and he never remarried. Slowly, Alzheimer's stole him away from us as well. I knew how much he loved the beach, loved to just sit by the ocean and watch the water, listen to the sound of the waves lapping at the sand. So, we took him to Rehoboth for what would be his last time. For the most part, he was lucid, but at times he resided somewhere else, somewhere in his memories, in his other world. To be honest, I was envious. He seemed happiest when he wasn't with us. I suspect when he was with Mom again in his mind.

When I took him to the Haunted Mansion, his eyes sparkled, and he grinned. He was my young father again.

The management had upgraded the Mansion over the past few years. When I visited the year before, the façade had a new paint job. The ride was smoother (they must have retooled the suspended track), and the gimmicks now all worked. My favorites were still there, maintaining the nostalgia of the place. Indeed, there were a few additions (like the ghoul that appeared to be "urinating" near the end of the ride), but all the familiar rooms were largely unchanged.

"You remember coming here, Pops? When I was a kid?"

He nodded. "Of course. The highlight of our summers."

"Do you want to ride it again, just for old-time's sake?"

"It's the main reason I came. Let's go!"

Dad had a little trouble getting into the car, and the ride attendant helped me get him situated. When the ride started, he leaned forward against the bar, anticipating what was to come.

"Dad, do you remember Melvin? The guy who took our tickets when we first went on the ride?"

"Sure. One ugly man. You thought he was a zombie."

"I still see him in the Mansion."

Dad turned to me. "Inside?"

"Yes. Usually standing in one of the rooms. Usually the Living Room."

"With the coffin and the pipe organ?"

"Right. I'm glad you remember."

"Son, that doesn't sound right. He'd be older than I am."

"I know. I don't think it's possible. But I still see him. Not every time, but …"

Dad stared at me for a moment. Then we entered the darkness, entered the Mansion for his last time. His attention went elsewhere.

Dad didn't jump when things popped out at him from the shadows. Like me, he'd been through the Mansion so many times there were no surprises. He pointed and laughed a few times, however, clearly enjoying himself.

We passed through the Graveyard, the room with the mad scientist and his monster, the hallway with the mounted heads, and the massive skull with the glowing red eyes. My father loved it all.

But when we entered the Living Room, Melvin was standing next to the fireplace, leaning against the grandfather clock in the corner. He didn't move, didn't appear to notice us at all. The car moved past the pile of skulls on the floor, the open coffin, and the ghoul at the pipe organ. I didn't look back this time. I was sure Melvin was no longer there.

"I love the pipe organ," Dad said.

"Sure, dad. I always liked that, too."

The car went around the corner, into a dark hallway.

"Who was that man back there?" Dad asked.

"You saw a man? You saw Melvin?"

"I don't know if it was Melvin. But I saw a man back there, standing next to the fireplace."

"So, you did see him!"

"But I don't know why your mother was there. She shouldn't have been there."

"You saw my mother?"

"You didn't see her waving at us?"

"Dad, she's been gone for ten years now."

He turned to me with a look of confusion.

I sighed. I now had no idea what he'd seen, if he'd seen anything at all. Or maybe I was the delusional one.

* * *

In the summer of 2000, when Ben was nine, he asked me to go to the Haunted Mansion. He'd taken a liking to the old B&W horror films—Boris Karloff in *The Mummy* and *Frankenstein*, Lon Chaney in *The Werewolf*, Bela Lugosi as Dracula, and especially *The Thing*. Quieter, more subtle horror movies of the past. He enjoyed them all. So, he was ready for his initiation at the Mansion.

As we traveled through the dark maze of rooms, I watched Ben, his sense of wonder, his infectious joy. I then understood why my father had taken me on the ride so many years ago. This wasn't just the Haunted Mansion, not just a boardwalk attraction. Far more than that. As my father had done with me, I relived that sense of discovery, the new experience, vicariously through Ben. Even more, this was a shared adventure between father and son. A rite of passage. I understand now. This was just as important for Ben as it was for me. Perhaps more so.

I wasn't surprised when I spotted Melvin standing at the back of the Graveyard, beside a gnarly black tree among the tombstones. He disappeared behind the tree as soon as I noticed him.

"What was that monster back there?" Ben asked.

I turned to him. "You saw a monster?"

"The one behind the tree. Was that a vampire? I couldn't tell."

"What did it look like?"

"Maybe a man dressed in black. But I only saw him for a second."

I nodded. "Probably one of the props. There are so many monsters moving around in here."

"I know. It's great!"

So, I wasn't the only one who saw Melvin.

After Ben and I got off the ride, I asked the teenager taking the tickets, "Do you know Melvin?"

The kid, no older than sixteen, stopped chewing his gum, trolling for a thought. "Nope. No idea."

Then I noticed the old guy in the ticket booth motioning me over. The man appeared to be in his late sixties, unshaven and looking like every carny I'd seen in my life. I stepped to the open door at the back of the booth. He continued selling the tickets but talked over his shoulder to me.

"You askin' about Melvin?"

"You've seen him?"

"Perty near every damn day. Where'd you see Melvin? I usually see him hangin' around the Living Room, near the organist."

"Wait, you've seen him? You've seen the ghost?"

The man turned to me, and then laughed until tears came to his eyes. "The way you go on, mister! Melvin never left. He don't work here no more. But this is his life. He never left."

"I don't understand."

"He ain't no ghost, mister."

He turned to the window to sell more tickets but continued talking.

"Melvin was always a little slow, plus he's mute. He has this condition called strabismus. At least I think that's what they call it. His eyes ain't straight. Not his fault, of course. But it creeped people out whenever he looked at them, so he avoided all eye contact and never looked folks straight in the eyes. 'Cause he couldn't. And, being mute, that made life even more difficult for him. He scared the kids most especially."

"I was afraid of him when I first saw him," I said. "I thought he was a zombie, just part of the show. And that was decades ago."

"Back when he was a ride attendant, sure. Back in the early seventies. Thing is, he loved kids. Melvin had a good heart and a kind soul. It's sad the kids always thought he was scary. He'd never hurt a one of 'em."

"But I still don't understand. I could swear I saw him just now. How can that be?"

"Melvin always loved the Mansion. Like I said, this is his life. So, we let him hang around, and he watches over the facilities. He don't work no more, no more paychecks. He retired long ago, got that Social Security and the Medicare. So, he's good. Lord, he must be in his seventies by now. Maybe eighty. But this is his home, so we let him stay. He even has a cot back there, case he wants to spend the night."

"Nobody on the ride notices him?"

"I'm sure they do. But I s'pect they think he's part of the show, ya know? See, you probably have this memory of him from years ago, right?"

"Yes, back when I was a kid."

"So, you recognize him. You remember him. Most don't. And he don't bother nobody. But a ghost? Well, not in the true sense of the word, no."

* * *

My grandson Justin screamed when the banshee leaped out at us, but he laughed after. He gripped my hand.

"That was scary, Pops!"

"But you weren't really scared, right? You know it's all make-believe."

"Sure, I know. It's just fun. Can we do it again when we're through?"

"You bet, kiddo. I've been riding this nearly every summer since I was your age."

And I was happy. I'd initiated another generation of the Rupert family into the simple joy that is the Haunted Mansion on the Rehoboth boardwalk.

As we came around a turn, I saw Melvin standing at the back of the Living Room. Just standing there, watching as our car went by. He looked good for a man pushing ninety. I don't think Justin noticed him. Or, if he did, he probably thought Melvin was a prop, part of the scenery. In a way, he was.

I waved to Melvin, just a turn of my hand and a nod.

He did not return the gesture.

But he did smile.

A LESS-THAN-GRATIFYING VACATION IN PARIS

"Guy Savoy was such an excellent suggestion," Jennifer said. "The aged beef paleron is exquisite."

"Isn't it, though? And the seared veal sweetbread," Liza said. "Oh my God, it is soooo good. And I rarely eat veal."

"And the confit leeks with truffle!"

"It's all a bit pricy though, don't you think?"

"Our husbands can afford it."

"So true."

The friends laughed.

A trip to Paris was perfect this time of year, and much needed. They'd planned such excursions each spring. Money was now never an issue. Their husbands were filthy rich. Fidelity, on the other hand, was always an issue.

They had no illusions. At one time, a decade before, they'd been trophy wives of their much older husbands. And they'd been skilled at being merely ornaments hanging on their husbands' arms at swanky social events, trained to smile appropriately and fawn over their men when the situation dictated it. They readily accepted this, as long as the money flowed. Their husbands wouldn't dare divorce them at the risk of losing half their estates.

Jennifer Tolson, who came from Boston stock, was attuned to high societal mores. Her husband, Stephen, also came from a wealthy Boston family. He was born into money. Not Kennedy money, but enough to launch his own successful biotech corporation in Silicon Valley. Jennifer was an attractive brunette with an air of elegance and sophistication about her. Her eyes were different colors, blue and brown, like David Bowie's, and her lips were thin, almost brittle. But she was a head-turner and played the "wife" role well.

In contrast, Elizabeth Richards came from an upper-middle-class family from Pittsburgh. She met her husband, Burt, at a marketing conference in Philadelphia. More specifically, at a bar near the conference center, followed by an extraordinary one-night stand. Liza, a redhead with a face painted with freckles, was somewhat plain in looks but had skills that far than compensated for her lack of beauty. That one night of passion had conquered Burt. After their marriage, he became the Marketing Director of Tolson Industries. Soon after that, he partnered with Stephen in the business, which proved to be ridiculously lucrative as the biotech industry garnered more significance in the American corporate landscape.

"Magnificent view from here," Liza said, looking out the window. "The Seine and the Louvre. Almost as good as the food."

"You know, we've only just begun to explore Paris. There is so much we haven't seen yet, and our vacation is nearly over," Jennifer said. "We must plan another excursion here someday. Maybe in a few years."

"That sounds wonderful. We can talk about it on our flight home."

A waiter approached their table. In English, he asked, "Would you ladies like more wine?"

"Yes," Jennifer said. "I'd like to try the Liber Pater Bordeaux, please."

"Any particular year?" the waiter said.

"Oh, you may choose, garçon," Liza said.

"Merci. I will select the best for you fine ladies."

Liza nodded toward the waiter as he walked away.

"What do you think? He's quite cute."

"Far too young," Jennifer said. "He wouldn't do at all."

"I suppose you're right."

"So, what project has stolen Burt from you this time? Another business trip to Hong Kong?"

"Tokyo, actually," Liza said.

"Wasn't that where—what was her name, Kiki or Tiki or something? Wasn't that where he hooked up with her?"

"Kiki, yes. But that wasn't Tokyo. That was Maui."

"Oh, that's right. Hawaii. It's a shame Kiki fell into that volcano. Incredibly sad." Jennifer smiled. She sipped her wine, looking over the glass rim at her friend, who smiled as well.

"And Stephen?" Liza said. "What has he been up to? I heard the market crash forced him to cut back on company expenditures."

"No, his company had enough cash reserves to weather the storm, thank God. I couldn't do with a cut in my allowance. And, of course, he had to have *some* money to keep his mistress happy. Her apartment doesn't come cheap."

"Do you know who she is yet?"

"No. But in time," Jennifer said.

"That last one was somewhat elusive, too," Liza said.

"Tiffany. She was a slippery one."

"Tiffany. What was she, like twenty? Burt is so predictable."

"Isn't he? I think he enjoys being a sugar daddy."

"Well, Jen, you're fifteen years younger than Stephen. He likes them young."

"I suppose. But it's almost tiresome at this point," Jennifer said. "Poor Tiffany. So sad, that hit-and-run accident."

"Did they ever apprehend the driver?" Jennifer smiled again.

"Good Lord, no. And she lingered so long in the hospital, too. I'm sure her death was a wonderfully unpleasant one." Liza smiled.

"What do you think? Should we live dangerously and order dessert?"

* * *

They left Guy Savoy (after more-than-generously tipping their waiter) and strolled along the Seine, joining the throng of other tourists, many of them Americans. Although the air was crisp, the evening sun played warmly on their faces. They found a bench on the riverfront and seated themselves to take in the magnificent view.

"I'm thinking of remodeling the kitchen," Jennifer said.

"Really?" Liza said. "Didn't you just do that a year or so ago?"

"Three years, actually. But you get so tired of walking into the same room, day after day. So boring. I'm thinking of mahogany cabinetry. What do you think? And Cippolino Ondulato marble countertops with matching flooring tiles."

"Sounds exquisite," Liza said. "But don't you think the dark marble and the mahogany will make the room too gloomy? I think I'd go with walnut cabinets."

"Ah, but you're not thinking of the lighting! I would redo all the lighting to accent the colors in the room."

"Oh, yes. Can't wait to see it."

"Well, Stephen can certainly afford it," Jennifer said. "Of course, we'll need to replace all the appliances as well. Especially that refrigerator. It needs to be cleaned, but it's just easier to buy a new one, you know?"

"I know exactly what you mean. Who wants to clean a refrigerator?"

"For sure, not me! And I'd prefer not to ask Amanda to do it again. You can't hire good help these days. They always want health insurance and all those other benefits. All the other folderols. Who wants to bother with all that headache?"

"Tell me about it," Liza said. "By the way, speaking of new things, I'm contemplating buying a new Porsche."

"I thought you loved your car. Why trade it in?"

"Who said anything about trading it in? Can't a girl have two Porsches?"

"True, true." Jennifer laughed. "We really are spoiled brats, aren't we?"

"Spoiled? We've earned every bit of this. Every bit. We're entitled to everything we have, and more."

* * *

The crowd around the two Fontaines de la Concorde was thinner than they'd expected—not that they would have complained. As the sun set, the fountain lights bloomed into illumination. Jennifer and Liza circled the fountains several times, admiring the statuary sculpted nearly two centuries before and the orchestrated colored lighting of the dancing water. No visit to Paris was complete without seeing the city's various fountains scattered throughout, but these were the ones that most attracted the tourists.

"Ah, the Luxor Obelisk," Liza said, pointing to the structure at the other end of the square, its spire jutting toward the clouds far above.

"It's like a miniature Washington Monument, isn't it?"

"I wouldn't tell a local citizen that."

"You're right. They would probably take offense."

"Can you imagine?" Liza said. "The obelisk marks the spot where the great guillotine stood during the French Revolution."

"How many hundreds of heads rolled here?" Jennifer said. "It must have been a bloody spectacle."

"People would come by the droves to watch the beheadings. The only entertainment of that day. I mean, there was no television back then, of course. No movies. It was a dull life until the chopping began."

"I wish I could have been there," Jennifer said.

"Well, knowing us, we'd have been the ones with the severed heads. I don't think we'd enjoy that much."

"We'd certainly have an audience, though."

"Yes, but no encore, and we wouldn't hear the applause. Well, not for long anyway," Liza said. "I think I'd rather perform in community theater."

"I've done that. I think a ride on the guillotine would be far more satisfying."

"True."

"You know, I hate leaving here tomorrow. Our vacation has been far too short. There is so much more to see, so much more to experience," Liza said.

"You know what we haven't done?"

"What's that?"

"Perfume," Jennifer said.

"Ooooh … you're right."

"We bought some fabulous jewelry at Castiglione Bijoux. That antique sapphire necklace you found, that's a one-of-a-kind piece. And gorgeous on you."

"And that diamond brooch you found," Liza said. "Marie Antionette could have worn it."

"But the perfume. We forgot the perfume!"

"I even had Maison Hayari on my list. You know, that's one of Nicole Kidman's favorite perfume shops here in Paris."

"And Beyoncé's," Jennifer said. "Anything good enough for Beyoncé is more than good enough for me."

"Well, maybe next visit. We're not going to have time now."

"Shame, really. But you're right. Next time."

The two women sat at the Maritime Fountain to start people-watching, one of their favorite pastimes when visiting cities around the world. That was the only genuine way to absorb the culture of a city, far more valuable than sightseeing. You can learn so much more from watching a street vendor than visiting a museum, the two friends thought.

"I think there are more tourists than Parisians," Liza said.

Jennifer nodded. "I think you're right. Too many gawkers."

"We need to find a local guy."

"Agreed."

"Check him out. There to the right of the obelisk, standing alone and taking pictures," Liza said.

Jennifer hesitated, tapping her bottom lip with a manicured nail. "I don't know. Looks like a tourist, too. Kind of a pretty boy, don't you think? Kind of prissy."

"You're right. Probably doesn't even prefer women. What about the other guy sitting on the bench alone?"

"The dark-haired man with the goatee?"

"That one, yes."

"He looks like your stereotypical Parisian artist. Something Matisse about him."

"So, yes or no?"

"Well, he reminds me of Burt," Jennifer said. "But you would know better than me."

"Slightly younger version, yes," Liza said. "I can see it, especially around the eyes."

"Well, we fly out tomorrow." Jennifer sighed. "We must decide."

"You're right, of course. We have limited time."

"Do you have the English-French dictionary?" Jennifer said. "How do you say, 'Want to party with us?'"

* * *

The next morning, Jennifer and Liza had seated themselves on the eleven-fifteen flight to Heathrow, a short layover before flying to the New York Kennedy Airport and then another layover before the flight to LAX. The sun shone brightly in a near-cloudless sky. They expected a pleasurable flight.

"Well, he didn't scream like the man last year in Rio," Jennifer said. "What was his name?"

"Enrique, I think," Liza said. "Maybe Enrico."

"Whatever."

"The ball gag definitely reduced the noise this time around. Excellent suggestion."

"But Francois wasn't much fun at all," Jennifer said. "I think the bastard may have even enjoyed it."

"True. And he lapsed into unconsciousness far too soon. I think we could have made a better choice."

"Ah, well. I must say, I truly enjoyed Paris. Did you know the death penalty doesn't exist in France? You can murder someone and totally get away with it."

They laughed in unison as the jet lifted from the tarmac.

"Of course, you could get life," Liza said. "And the French prisons aren't exactly like a stay at the Hilton."

Jennifer nodded. "It's a shame we must leave Paris so soon. It's such a lovely city."

"So, where should we go next year?"

"Well, we already have the English-French dictionary," Jennifer said. "And I hear Montreal is gorgeous in the spring."

DUNES

There was snow on the beach, dunes upon dunes, and the ocean, pissed at the world, clawed at the surf with icy fingers.

James gazed out over the bitter Atlantic from his tenth-floor hotel room window. He'd checked into the hotel the previous evening, in the middle of the worst nor'easter to hit the Northeast seaboard in decades. The trip from Atlanta to Atlantic City had been pure hell.

James saw white caps on the waves as far out as he could see. The wind howled like a demon outside the window. He wanted to see dolphins. Even seagulls. Any form of life. But the water and the beach were barren.

He wanted summer again.

Hard to believe that, only months before, James had brought the family to this very hotel, this beach, for a week of sun and fun. He remembered Luke and Matt, six and eight, helping him build an enormous sandcastle and then gleefully pounding it back into the sand with their bare feet. James could hear Matt laughing as they both attempted to boogieboard on the chaotic waves, often tumbling together in the surf and chasing their boards in the wet sand. He remembered telling both boys to stop throwing potato chips to the hordes of raucous gulls that surrounded their beach blanket.

Most of all, James remembered the distinct aroma of cocoa butter, the sweet suntan lotion on Lori's bronze skin as she soaked up the sun, stretched out next to him on the blanket. She turned to him, a magnificent smile for him, a gift. He so loved this woman. She was beautiful beyond description, beyond imagination. James felt like the luckiest man on the planet, right at that moment when she smiled for him.

Was that really the last time she smiled?

James wanted summer again.

But seasons change.

There was snow on the sand, dunes upon dunes, and James was due in divorce court at noon.

DEERMAN

The man wore camouflage attire in the tree stand, a good fifteen feet above the forest floor. The camouflage was ridiculous, better suited for Fallujah than a forest in upstate New York. I could smell the beer on his breath from a mile away. He looked to be nodding off, on the brink of sleep, his rifle resting across his knees. What a doofus. He had no clue I was there, aiming at him with a Glock 43 rigged with a SKYBEN Olight Baldar Mini tactical flashlight—perfect for zeroing in on a cranium.

I trained the small, blue bead of light on his forehead, holding it there in the hope he would open his eyes and realize he was in the crosshairs. I love plugging 'em with their eyes bugged, mouth wide, as they realized a bullet was coming. But he never looked up. In fact, he started snoring. I waited another two minutes, got bored, figured screw it, and plugged him anyway. He toppled from the stand headfirst, slamming into the leaf-blanketed ground at the tree's base.

Another one down.

So many more to go. Seems like more every year.

Deer season had arrived!

I trotted to where the man's body rested, folded like a broken marionette, arms akilter and legs obscenely bent. There wasn't much left of the back of his head. It was a clean kill. Well, not so much clean … but you know what I mean. One and done.

I couldn't linger. Rutting season was in full swing, and I'd seen a good many does prancing among the trees. I had a job to do and didn't need the distraction. But you had to deal with natural urges from time to time.

They call us venison. What should I call them, other than idiots? What would they taste like? I heard pork. Of course, I have no idea what pork tastes like either. I'm a vegetarian.

I looked at his rifle, just a few feet away from his corpse. It was a Remington Sendero, a standard deer-hunting rifle. Had a nice scope, too—utterly wasted on this buffoon. I debated on taking the rifle but decided not. My two Glocks were all I needed.

I've been on a vigilante campaign ever since Bambi's mother ate a bullet. Enough is enough, ya know? Something had to be done. That's when my crusade began.

As I stood there, admiring my hoofiwork, an arrow whistled just above my shoulder, nicking the hide as it passed. I didn't see the man with the bow, didn't even smell him.

Too risky. I had to move and dashed for the deeper brush.

* * *

Bowhunters are the worst! My buddy, Dodger, took an arrow to his flank. It might have been better to take him out with a direct hit to the heart. But, no, the killer missed. The bowhunters, two of the bastards, followed Dodger for miles before the pain, loss of blood, and fatigue finally got the best of my friend. The hunters finished him when they found him.

Poor Dodger didn't live up to his name, unfortunately. I'm guessing his head, with his ten-point rack, is mounted on a den wall somewhere, probably over a fireplace, staring into oblivion.

The two hunters? Nah, they weren't so skilled at dodging either. I had some fun with them. Wish I had a wall to mount *their* heads on.

* * *

I always thought of myself as a superhero. You know. Deerman. I'd spent years learning my craft, perfecting my firearms and fighting skills. Deerman! Of course, I'm not a man (thank God). And I'd be a superhero with no alter ego, much less a cape. I mean, my alter ego would be a *deer*. How dumb is that?

My father started me on my quest for vengeance. He first taught me how to defend myself. It took years just to master guns. He preferred a Sig Sauer P229. I was more comfortable with a Glock 43. That whole hooves thing. Pretty tricky.

Pops was the epitome of patience. He made me who I am. I enjoyed all the time my father and I spent in our training sessions. He excelled at taekwondo, but I could never get the hang of it. I just didn't have the physique and flexibility for it. Pops was lean and mean.

I never had a chance to learn knifework from him, despite his mastery with blades. A redneck driving a dilapidated Chevy Silverado pickup truck took Pops out. Blinded by the headlights, he never had a chance. I know, the "deer-in-the-headlights" cliché. I was devastated and my mother never got over it. I was even more determined to rid the forest of the scourge.

Damn humans.

* * *

The forest is so tranquil in the early morning, just as the sun rises. Peaceful. Quiet. Leaves whispering in a gentle breeze. The soft murmur of water flowing over the pebbles of a stream bed. The sweet sound of songbirds, invisible in the thick branches of the trees. This side of heaven.

What a crock!

The forest is filled with horrors, the realm of predators and prey. Potential death waits behind every tree. Every rabbit, every squirrel, lives in perpetual terror. The screech of a hawk above could be the last thing they hear.

My home.

Then add humans bearing weapons to the wonderful woods.

Fun, huh?

No wonder I love kicking hunter ass!

* * *

I heard the bow hunter behind me. Sounded like only one of them and, like most humans, he was anything but stealthy. More like bumbling and stumbling—lethal, nonetheless. I had to stay on the move. Given that he missed me when I was motionless, he was like an inept hunter, maybe one new to the game. I'd possibly end up like Dodger with an arrow in my ass if I couldn't evade him.

But I had the element of surprise. The man had probably never faced a stag with dual firearms.

I made my way through the tightly clustered trees, maneuvers I learned long ago. I knew every turn, every hiding place in the woods. My size made this extremely difficult. Hiding wasn't the answer to evading the hunters. Best to stay on the move until I could develop a strategy for taking them out.

I then no longer heard the man behind me. I paused, frozen still and listening. Nothing. And I could no longer smell him. A hunter had placed a scent lure nearby, its odor overpowering any trace of a human. I stood motionless, trying to determine where the man was. If a deer can do anything, standing without flinching a muscle is instinctive. Half the time, a hunter could walk right past you, unaware you stood close by blending into the background.

Where was this guy? He couldn't have been too far behind me.

The scent lure was horrendously pungent. I mean, I squat and piss on my legs to attract the females. You know, what humans call rub-urinating. Gets nasty, but the girls seem to dig it. So, I can't complain. The scent lures used by these hunters? I don't know, maybe humans use actual deer urine to make this stuff. Which begs the question: How the hell would humans collect deer piss? What kind of dedication to hunting would be required to squeeze deer bladders? And the scent lures are so *off.* Like the piss was a noxious brew of bear, raccoon, and skunk urine. Never attracted me, but the stench always told me the human idiots were in the area.

The odor was especially potent in this part of the forest. So, I knew one of the cretins was nearby.

I saw the hunter too late and had no time to react. This man was a step up from the usual dimwits I encountered. How had he been so quiet? He'd been so loud earlier, making his way through the woods. And the scent lure effectively masked his smell because I hadn't detected that aggressive human odor. Or beer. Or, occasionally, Old Spice.

The arrow speared my left flank, and I feared I'd just been "dodgered." As the hunter approached, I acted surprised, whipping my head as if in fear, and then dropped to my rear haunches. There surprisingly little pain, but I wanted the hunter to think it was excruciating.

As the human neared, he lifted his bow and notched another arrow, preparing to deliver the coup de grâce.

That's when I hefted my two Glocks. I smiled at the bewildered expression on his face before I pulled the triggers simultaneously. His head blossomed like a gorgeous crimson peony. A clean kill … well, again, you know what I mean.

I had to deal with the arrow in my ass. The arrow had passed through fat, not muscle, in my flank. That's why the pain was minimal. I still had to remove the projectile, and the barbed tip would do more damage if I tried to pull it out. The only option was to drive it through.

I backed up to a tree and started thwacking my butt against its trunk, forcing the arrow deeper and deeper until the barbed tip pierced the skin on the other side of my flank. I snapped off the arrow's tip with my teeth and reversed the shaft back through my flesh. Not fun, but easy enough.

I heard another hunter coming down the path to my right. Presumably, the dead guy's hunting buddy. They always seem to travel in pairs. Sometimes three or four together. They considered this a "sport." How ridiculous is this, killing my innocent, defenseless brethren? A sport? Well, I made their sport a tad more interesting.

I then saw the man, who also carried a bow. He lifted the weapon. He'd seen me. Time to run again. I wove through the tangled brush and stopped near a thick oak to watch. The hunter turned to see his fallen comrade, and I heard him gasp. He approached the dead man, turning left and right as if he expected an attack. He had to assume another human had killed the man. The man would never suspect an assassin deer.

He jerked his head up and somehow saw me through the trees. I always found it difficult to read human faces, but I recognized this—anger. Maybe fear, I couldn't tell. Nope, anger, without a doubt. He raised the bow again. Could he suspect I'd killed the man? Impossible.

I ran.

While dealing with the arrow in my ass, I'd dropped the damn Glocks! I mean, my grip on the guns was tenuous to begin with—you know, the hooves and all. Dropping them was an enormous mistake. I was weaponless and could do nothing now but run. I never saw a third hunter, so I assumed this was the only one who remained. When this was over, I'd backtrack to find the guns. I didn't want to lose those beauties. No hurry, however.

The hunter was distracted, not aware I hid in the thicket outside the clearing in which he stood. He was looking in the opposite direction, his back to me. He reloaded his bow, notching an arrow and pulling back the bowstring.

That's when I noticed the doe thirty yards away, her head bent to the ground, grazing on clover. It was Clarisse, one of my favorites! She didn't see the hunter as he lifted and sighted his bow.

I charged, ripping through the brush. The hunter spun toward me, too late. My rack speared into him. I tossed my head back, sending him flying over my shoulders and into a nearby tree. Despite dropping his crossbow, he still wasn't finished. As he stood, I kicked with my back legs. A hoof to the head is not quite as much fun as pumping a bullet through a human skull. But it was still mighty effective. And certainly more satisfying. His head splattered like a smashed melon, spraying a lovely blood pattern on the tree behind him. It was almost a work of art.

Clarisse approached me, smiling the way only a doe can. She nudged my neck and had that certain glow in her eyes. She clearly wanted to show her gratitude. My campaign of hunting the hunters could wait another day. Besides, I needed to take a break from the fun and games.

It was time to do a doe!

TO SEE THE ELEPHANT

Gettysburg, July 1, 1863

"I saw the elephant," the soldier said. Dr. Jeremiah Camfield thought the boy's eyes would explode from their sockets, his eyes were so wide. He realized the agony the soldier suffered, surely causing delirium.

"Yes, you've seen battle …"

"No, you don't understand. I saw the elephant. *Saw* it!"

"Son, we must attend to your wounds."

The soldier seemed not to hear him. "Last night. It was huge, moving through the battlefield. Moving over the bodies. Dead men, everywhere. Everywhere!"

The boy was no older than sixteen and a conical chunk of lead, a Minié ball, had shattered his life. The bullet struck his knee, exploding it into a mass of ruptured flesh, blood, and splintered bone. Camfield knew he'd have to amputate the leg just above the joint, mid-thigh. He thought it would have been more humane to slit the boy's throat.

The Minié ball caused the most damage that Camfield had ever seen done to a human body. The lucky victims were those shot in an arm or a leg. This usually led to amputation, but at least they'd survive. Well, unless infection set in, which was far too often. A Minié ball to the head or torso was sure death.

Camfield was just a country doctor, a general practitioner accustomed to doling out herbal remedies (which he considered placebos), caring for sick children, delivering babies—everything a doctor would commonly do in a small town like Duncanville, Georgia, his hometown.

Gettysburg was far removed from that life, a life he desperately wanted again. But he'd been conscripted into the Confederate Army. His medical expertise, as limited as it was, was required on the front lines. He'd witnessed firsthand the horrors of war and wanted nothing more to do with it. Here, they used a barn as a makeshift field hospital. It smelled of blood, gangrenous and rotting flesh, and cow shit. Camfield knew the stench would linger in his nostrils—or at least his memory—for the rest of his life.

The boy writhed on the table, a wooden door straddling two sawhorses. He howled in pain like an animal. Two other soldiers, not much older, held the boy down at the shoulders. Another man held down his legs.

Three other soldiers with ravaged bodies lay on blankets nearby on the dirt floor of the barn, waiting for their turn under the knife. Ironically, they were the lucky ones. They had been triaged and brought to the field hospital for immediate treatment. Many others with less severe injuries waited outside the barn, not to receive medical attention at all. If time allowed, Camfield could tend to all those injured. Time never allowed. After each battle, he stood for endless hours over the operating table as a line of gravely injured and dying men—and now children—passed under his scalpel and bone saw. His frustration and anger grew as the hours slogged by, for he knew his efforts were often useless and senseless.

The day before, another delirious soldier was brought screaming into the makeshift operating room. The man claimed to have seen a massive monster on the battlefield, something from a nightmare that drove the man mad. In his delirium, he'd stabbed Camfield's fellow surgeon several times in the gut, killing him. This left Camfield with no medical assistance. He was on his own, like many other doctors in many other barns surrounding the massive battlefield.

The hysterical soldier committed suicide later that day.

Considering all the cannon fire, gunfire, and unrelenting screaming, Camfield was sure the battle would rage through the next day and beyond. And he was already exhausted. He understood, to some degree, why the soldier had killed himself. The war ravaged everyone eventually, even those who survived.

Camfield leaned over the boy, putting his hand gently on the boy's forehead. The boy was feverish, shivering. The doctor would have to act expeditiously. Despite the tourniquet on the boy's leg, he'd lost a great deal of blood.

"What's your name, son?"

The boy appeared confused, as if Camfield had spoken another language.

"I'm going to help you as best I can. Understand?" He leaned closer to the boy's ear. "What's your name, son?"

He called them all his sons. He was old enough to be their father, most of them were so young. War was not a place for teenagers. Or a place for any sane human.

"Johnny." The boy gritted his teeth between white lips, as if merely speaking his name brought agony. "Johnny Hansford."

"My name is Jeremiah," Camfield said. "People often call me Jeremy."

He touched the boy's shoulder, knowing it was faint comfort. Hansford had already closed his eyes.

The camp had run out of ether and chloroform the day before when the Confederate forces arrived at Gettysburg. Medical supplies had dwindled because of the Union blockades. Camfield could not anesthetize the boy. He had one option. He turned to the other soldiers.

"There, on the floor. That small, broken piece of wood."

"Sir?" the soldier to his right said.

"The wood. Put it between his teeth."

The three soldiers looked at him in horror.

"We don't have time," Camfield said. "Hurry."

"You're not gonna put 'im out? Anesthesia?" one of them asked.

Camfield ignored the question. "The wood. Put it in his mouth. Now!"

One of them put the eight-inch piece of wood between Hansford's teeth. The boy's eyes flared open.

"Bite down, son," Camfield said. "Bite down hard, as hard as you can. Good. And close your eyes again. Do you have a girl at home? I'm sure you do, a handsome man like yourself."

Johnny nodded.

"I bet she's pretty."

Johnny nodded again.

"Keep your eyes closed and think about her. You'll be seeing her soon." Camfield knew it was likely a lie. But if it brought any comfort to the boy, he was more than willing to lie.

He looked at the other soldiers. "We need to hurry now. I need you men to hand me my tools immediately as I ask for them. Understand?"

The three nodded, but all appeared dumbfounded and crippled with horror.

Camfield pointed to the tray of bloodied instruments at the foot of the table. "Hand me the scalpel. Yes, yes! That blade there."

He snatched the scalpel from the man's hand, ignoring the possibility of injuring himself. He made an incision above the knee, sliding the blade through the skin and muscle, slicing to the bone, and leaving a flap of skin. The boy groaned and thrashed.

"Hold him, dammit!"

Camfield used the bone saw with precision, hoping to make the procedure quick. The boy passed out soon after the sawing began. Just as well, Camfield thought. At least Hansford didn't vomit into his own throat, a reaction the doctor often faced during surgery. He severed the leg and tossed it onto the pile of limbs in a far corner of the barn. He swiftly tied off the arteries. After smoothing over the jagged edge of the bone with his blade, he folded the skin flap over the end of the stump and sutured it closed.

"Hold his leg up," Camfield said to the soldier on the other side of the table. "Good, that's high enough." He applied isinglass plaster to the stump and then bandaged it with a roll of filthy gauze.

"We're finished," he said to the three men. He pointed to a cot between two other amputees who were also unconscious. "Move him over there. Careful now! Careful. The plaster needs to set."

After attending to the boy, the soldiers brought in the next injured man and placed him on the table. It amazed Camfield the man was still alive. A bullet had entered above his left eye and exited his skull just behind the left ear. The skull there was splintered like a dropped vase. Camfield assumed the bullet somehow skated along the interior of the skull over the left lobe, leaving minimal damage to the brain. How was that even possible?

"I feel fine, doc," the soldier said as Camfield packed the wound, front and back, with gauze. "Not even a headache."

"You're a lucky man," Camfield said.

"I wouldn't go that far, but at least I ain't dead."

Not yet, Camfield thought. The wound was inflamed and showed signs of pus, already infected. He knew such head wounds proved fatal. The man was doomed.

Then the doctor moved to the next patient.

* * *

The night came hard for Camfield, sleeping on a cot in a corner of the barn, his back aching from standing all day. The morning would come too soon, and he desperately needed rest.

Strange how quiet the night was, despite the violence and death from the preceding day. Thousands of men lay dying or dead in the surrounding fields. Many dead lay just outside the barn, men he could not attend to, let alone save. His medical expertise had been stressed to the limit, to the point of exhaustion. Tomorrow would be no different.

There came a rustling from the far corner of the barn, near the pile of amputated body parts. No one had the time to bury the legs and arms, and they'd begun to rot and draw vermin and flies. Camfield remained still, listening. Yes, he heard movement in the straw over there. He'd seen rats in the barn earlier. They took advantage of the darkness to feast. The rustling came again, louder this time.

He reached for the gas lantern nearby. He pulled a match from his shirt pocket and flicked it to spark with his thumbnail. The sound stopped. He lit the lamp and held it high to see the barn floor. Nothing. No movement. No sound. Nothing. Had it been his imagination, a fragment of a dream?

Johnny Hansford slept on a cot near the barn door. The other soldiers on whom Camfield had performed surgery the previous day had been moved to the tents outside. Only the boy remained in the barn with him.

Camfield then heard a scratching, scraping sound. He sat up and turned the lamp again toward the heap of arms and legs. He thought he saw several fingers on a severed hand flex and pull the hand across the floor, moving like an insect, and then stop. A trick of the light?

He stood and approached the hand. It lay still. He pushed it with the toe of his boot. Nothing. Just a lifeless hand. He picked it up, examined it, and then tossed it on top of the heap of ruined flesh. Had to have been his imagination, on the edge of sleep.

Camfield returned to his bed, still staring at the hand. He shook his head. If he now imagined crawling hands, he definitely needed sleep. He extinguished the lantern and reclined onto the cot. Exhaustion finally drove Camfield into a fitful sleep filled with nightmares of endless war and rivers of blood.

July 2, 1863

At dawn, cannon fire ripped Camfield from sleep. He rubbed his eyes, rolled to the side of the cot, and then sat on its edge. The air was hot and fetid already, and the stench of blood, burnt gunpowder, and decomposing flesh hovered like a mist above the ground outside the open door of the barn. The horrors had begun anew.

He would sell his soul for a decent cup of coffee. And he almost preferred to starve than to eat another piece of hardtack or salt horse. Even clean, potable water was scarce here.

He turned to the boy on the cot, intending to check his condition, when he noticed the corner of the barn was empty. All the severed limbs had vanished in the night. Only bloodstained straw remained. How could that be? He must have been deep in sleep when someone cleared the entire area.

There were two barn doors. The front led to the Confederate encampment, to his patients. The other, at the rear of the barn, led to the battlefield. It was now open, although it had been closed earlier.

The first soldier of the morning entered the barn through the front entrance, carrying fresh gauze, bandages, and towels. Camfield had no idea where the man had found the supplies.

Camfield pointed to where the severed limbs had been. "Did the men take everything away during the night while I slept?"

"Why, no, sir." The man seemed puzzled. "No one has been in here, to my knowledge."

"Someone *must* have moved them."

"No, sir."

"To bury them?"

"No, sir."

"Surely someone had to. As you can see, they are gone." He pointed toward the rear barn door. "Why is that open?"

The soldier shrugged.

"No one opened the barn door?" Camfield said. He approached it and latched it shut.

"No, sir."

Camfield scratched the back of his head, staring at the empty corner of the barn. Was he losing his mind? This damnable war. It would destroy them all. He turned back to the soldier.

"Well, thank you for bringing the fresh supplies. Did we receive any ether or chloroform?"

"No, sir. We're not even getting enough food for our troops."

"You're dismissed, then."

Camfield had heard the stories shared by some soldiers. In the utter darkness of the night on other battlefields, beyond the illumination of the campfires and oil lanterns, something moved across the land scattered with corpses. It moved unseen. And, on the following mornings, they found that many body parts of fallen soldiers had disappeared in the night.

Scavengers? He'd heard of massive wolves in the area, and carrion birds always circled above the battlefields. He supposed foxes and raccoons, maybe even feral dogs and cats, would feed on the fresh meat.

But the numbers didn't add up. Thousands perished in this battle alone. It would take an army of scavengers to steal away so many body parts. Too many. It was impossible.

Camfield looked at the bloodied straw where the amputated arms and legs had been piled the day before. He shivered. Something even more monstrous than the war was here.

Camfield tended to Hansford. Just as he feared, the boy had developed a high-grade fever. The boy had pyemia and rapidly approached sepsis. Camfield also knew he could do nothing to stop it, and the mortality rate was near one hundred percent. The boy lingered under a death sentence. It seemed every man who came into this barn faced the same end. Perhaps even Camfield himself.

A soldier entered the makeshift hospital with the first patient of the day, a man in a blue uniform. Blood soaked the man's left side, likely a gunshot grazing wound to the abdomen.

"What is this?" Camfield asked the man in gray.

"A Union deserter. He crossed the line during the night and somehow made it across the battlefield. He was delirious when he reached our camp, frightened beyond imagination, and we almost shot him. But he was pleading for help."

"I saw the elephant last night," the Union soldier said. His voice was weak, barely a whisper. "Bigger than an elephant. The darkness was so deep. A massive shape moving across the field. Never slowing. A monster."

"Monster?" Camfield assumed the man suffered from battle fatigue and had hallucinated whatever he'd seen, much like Hansford and the suicidal soldier from the day before.

"I don't know what else to call it. A monster. Don't know where it came from or where it was going. Only know that it disappeared into the darkness as I hugged the ground."

Camfield examined the man's wound—indeed, a gunshot wound, but not critical. Other soldiers with more serious wounds waited outside the barn. The doctor applied a temporary bandage. Camfield hated triaging patients, but he had to tell the soldier he'd have to wait for treatment, perhaps later in the day. If at all.

Camfield's day progressed as he'd expected. Soldier after ruined soldier. The war raged a mere hundred yards from the barn, the cannon fire often shaking the foundation of the building and making his surgery even more perilous. He needed a steady hand. Considering his exhaustion, he wondered how he could lift his hands at all.

By the afternoon, the heap of severed limbs was piled higher than it had been the previous day. He couldn't imagine how horrified the injured soldiers must be when they were brought into the barn and saw so many bloodied arms and legs, knowing they would soon contribute to the nightmarish collection. Camfield thought the delirious ones were luckier. They had no sense of what was to come.

The Hansford boy died early that evening as the sun set, never regaining consciousness. Another victim of pyemia. Another of thousands of casualties. For the best, Camfield thought. He asked several soldiers to carry the boy to the pile of other corpses in an adjacent field—human detritus to be dealt with later. The men had more to worry about—keeping their own lives, much less caring for the dead.

As darkness fell, the battle waned … but never ended. Camfield knew it would continue into the night, then eventually diminish enough so he could get some sleep. He'd welcome even an hour or two.

July 3, 1863

Long after midnight, Camfield awoke with a start and sat up on his cot. The rustling, scratching noise in the straw was much louder this time, an angry sound in Camfield's mind. He sat for a moment in the darkness, listening. There were no injured soldiers in the barn that night. All had been moved to nearby tents and other shelters. Tonight, he was alone in the building.

The sound intensified. Whatever it was, he sensed the beast was enormous. Scratching. Clawing at the ground. But, oddly, there were no grunting noises, no squeals, no animal vocalizations of any kind. What was this thing?

He reached for the lantern, then hesitated. Did he really want to see what was happening? What sort of animal—or animals—could consume so many severed limbs?

Camfield thought of escaping, of fleeing whatever it was. The southern barn door, the one that led to his fellow soldiers and the one through which he'd hoped to escape, was closed. He'd have to unlatch the door to pass through it, and in that instant perhaps the animal could pounce on him. The northern door, also latched, led to the battlefield. He dared not open that one, knowing what lay beyond.

His hand hovered over the lantern. He had to know. God help him, he had to know.

He lit the lantern and raised it above his head.

There was no animal, no scavenger.

The entire heap of bloodied limbs had coalesced, circling, pulling pieces of itself together, melding parts to form a growing entity. Hands and feet moved in unison, pulling the ball together as it rotated, picking up stray body parts as it did so. Elbows and knees bent and flexed, helping the globular thing mold itself into a sphere.

Camfield could only stare in horror, his heart pounding in his chest. What thing from hell was this?

The monstrous sphere stopped moving, resting on the straw-strewn ground. All the body parts on the barn floor had been subsumed, the parts pulled together in a completed puzzle of death. In the lantern's light, Camfield could see the ball of flesh pulsing, as if it had a heartbeat. Then Camfield understood. This was the embodiment of the war, this living thing possessed of dead flesh. This sphere comprised all the blood, the pain, the fear, the needless death of the battlefield.

The thing was at least ten feet tall, Camfield guessed, reaching the barn's rafters. It gradually turned and rolled toward the latched northern barn door, picking up speed as it went. The sphere struck the door, splintering it at the hinges, but not breaking free. The thing rolled backward, then rammed forward again, this time wrenching the door from its hinges and toppling it to the ground. The sphere rolled across the fallen door, stopped, and turned, hesitating as if surveying the battlefield still littered with corpses.

Camfield rose from his cot, still holding the lantern high. Whatever this thing was, it paid him no attention. But his fear had not subsided.

The sphere then rolled onto the battlefield, picking up body parts as it went, doubling in size as Camfield watched. Hundreds of dead soldiers contributed to its girth, growing and growing as it traversed the bloodied ground.

He stepped to the barn door as the massive ball of mounting flesh moved into the distance, soon out of the range of his lantern. He could sense the movement in the darkness. Then it was gone.

Camfield now understood the true horror of this godforsaken war.

He'd seen the elephant.

HEARING MILDRED

Mildred Mayfield died of a ruptured aortic aneurysm on the cold eve of Easter. She'd left her Easter Sunday best spread out on the bed in the guest bedroom. Harold, her husband, figured she'd been thinking of him, not church—what better clothes to bury her in? Mildred was always so thoughtful, Harold thought. If she didn't tell him what to do, she did it for him.

* * *

"Dad, we need to talk," William said. He sat on the couch opposite Harold's recliner in the living room. As always, the TV was tuned to an old cops show.

Harold never called his son, his only child, William. He would always be Billy to him. But it didn't seem right to call his fifty-five-year-old son Billy.

"I already know what you're going to say, Billy."

Harold smiled a bit when he saw his son wince at the name.

"Dad, you're eighty-two. Mom's been gone for six months. You can't stay in this house by yourself."

"Why not? I've lived here for five decades. Your mother would not want me to leave our home."

"What if something happens to you? Jen and I live an hour away."

"There's always 911."

"What if you can't get to the phone?"

"Then I can't get to the phone. So what? I just want to sit in my comfortable recliner, occasionally with a good Scotch, and watch TV."

"All day long?"

"Of course. What, am I going to go play tennis? Go drag racing? Chase skirts? I'm eighty-two. Meals on Wheels keeps me fed. I see no reason to leave the house, Billy. None."

William sighed and shook his head.

* * *

Harold loved watching police shows and old mystery shows when he could find them on TV, typically late at night on three-digit cable networks. He spent hours watching shows like *Mannix*, *Ironside*, *Perry Mason*, *Hawaii Five-0*, and even the old *Dragnet* episodes. His favorite was *Matlock*. Harold looked a lot like Andy Griffith, and he could easily imagine himself in the scenarios Matlock often found himself in during each show.

One night, an episode of *Baretta*, starring Robert Blake, was scheduled for two a.m. on channel 306, whatever network that was. Harold had no TV-watching routine, other than stalking the channel scroll for viewing candidates. He didn't care much for sitcoms (just *I Love Lucy* and *The Honeymooners* plots regurgitated ad nauseam), so it was often difficult to find anything of interest.

As the theme song for *Baretta* began, Harold turned up his hearing aids. He couldn't hear a damn thing without them, even when the TV was at full volume. This time, static filled his hearing aids, so much that he couldn't hear the dialogue on the television. It wasn't so much static, he realized, as it was murmuring, distant conversation with no discernible words. Unintelligible chatter. "What the hell!"

Harold switched off the TV with the remote and listened. Yes, there were voices. He could hear voices, talk of some kind. But he couldn't make out the words.

He pulled out the hearing aids and placed them on the coffee table. Nothing. He couldn't hear a thing, so he put the hearing aids back in. He again heard the same noise, like a radio program just out of range. Voices, but not voices. Something else …

"Damn things are defective!"

He tried adjusting the volume on the hearing aids, to no avail.

Then, he distinctly heard his name, *HAROLD*, spoken with clarity through the mindless chatter. It was so sudden, so unexpected, that he yanked out both devices and tossed them on the table.

He definitely heard his name spoken.

And it was definitely his dead wife who'd spoken it.

* * *

The following day, soon after getting out of bed, Harold made a cup of coffee, turned on the TV in the living room, settled into his favorite recliner, and put in his hearing aids. No static, no murmuring. The hearing aids worked perfectly—the Weather Channel came through loud and clear.

Harold shrugged. He must have been just hearing things before.

* * *

A week passed before Harold heard his wife's voice through his hearing aids again. He was watching the latest iteration of *Hawaii Five-0* (not the same without Jack Lord!) when the static began. This time, he turned down the TV volume, closed his eyes, and just listened.

Whispering. Not quite intelligible, but almost, coming through the noise.

"Mildred?" he said aloud.

The noise became louder, more intense, irritating.

hear

Harold kept his eyes closed and kept silent.

hear

hard

He was pretty sure it was Mildred's voice.

hard to

"Is it you, Mildred?"

hear me

"I can—"

hard to get

"—hear you."

hard to get through

"I can hear you, Mildred. I can hear you! Where are you?"

The static was getting too loud.

here

And then he heard nothing but white noise.

* * *

William spread pamphlets and brochures across the kitchen table in front of his father.

"What's this?" Harold asked.

"I just brought them for you to look through. They're from retirement homes I'd recommend. We should visit a few, get a feel for what they offer."

"Not interested."

"Dad, you seriously need to consider your options."

"I have."

"Well, I particularly like Shady Oaks. The facility is clean and the folks there are very nice. Plenty of activities. Great food. I think you'd like it there if you gave it a chance."

"Not interested."

"Dad, you can be so stubborn at times! Well, I'll leave these here for you. Maybe you'll want to read them later."

* * *

Harold

"I'm here, Mildred."

it's hard

"What's hard?"

getting through ... takes all my strength

"Where are you?"

here with you

"I've missed you so much."

I know

Her voice was barely a whisper. Harold turned up the hearing aids, but the static made it difficult.

"Do you miss me?"

I've been here

"Why can't I see you?"

can't … manifest

"What?"

not strong

"I don't understand. Manifest?"

mani … ong enough

"I don't understand, Mildred."

weak

 "You know I love you."

know

Then there was only static.

* * *

Harold had no idea how she had contacted him. He was only pleased that she did. Was she actually haunting the house? Or was she talking to him from the other side? She said she was "here"—but where is "here"? No matter. He was happy to have Mildred in his life again.

They had talked off and on for days, and she seemed to get stronger and better able to communicate with him. He did not understand the barriers, what made it so difficult for her, and wished he could help in some way. He'd never believed in the paranormal, yet now it had become a mainstay in his life.

"Mildred, are you here?"

right here

"Can you see me?"

yes

"Why are you here?"

You need me

Harold nodded. He did need her.

why do you watch television so much

"I enjoy it. Now that I'm retired, I just want to kick back and relax. I started working on my father's farm when I was fourteen, and worked hard every year after until I retired at seventy-five. Now, I finally have time to do the thing I enjoy most. Watching TV."

The noise in his hearing aids dissipated, usually a sign that she was losing her strength and could no longer communicate with him. Her voice became a whisper.

but there's so much to do

"Do?"

around the house

* * *

"I wish we could go out to dinner together, like old times."

that would be nice

"I wish I could see you again."

I know

"Are you happy where you are?"

I'm here

"Are you happy?"

I'd be happier if you didn't watch TV so much

* * *

"But I do vacuum the house, Mildred."

every week

"No, not every week. Maybe once a month. I don't see a need to do it more often."

you must vacuum every week

* * *

"Mildred, I'm watching an episode of *McCloud*. Do you have any idea how hard it is to find an episode of *McCloud*?"

not important

"It's important to me."

there are more important things

"Such as?"

the kitchen won't paint itself

"I'm watching my show now."

why must you disappoint me

* * *

"I'm not doing that right now."

the trash needs to go out

"I'm watching TV. I'll do it in the morning."

you'll forget to do it in the morning ... do it now

"Leave me alone, Mildred."

do it now

* * *

nothing is getting done around this house

* * *

look at the dust ... can't you see the dust

* * *

you are the most lazy, inconsiderate man I know

* * *

After tolerating several weeks of endless nagging, Harold took another tack.

"Mildred, we were married for fifty-two years. More than half a century. You were my high-school sweetheart, the love of my life. But, darlin', you have to understand. You're dead. You died over six months ago.

It's time for you to move on. Go to the light. Go get your heavenly reward. And, for the love of God, leave me the hell alone!"

At first, Harold thought maybe she'd left him. The quiet was almost oppressive. Maybe she understood, finally. Maybe she had moved on after all. A minute went by, and then two.

Mildred whispered.

there's so much to do around the house

Harold sighed.

the kitchen needs to be painted ... you promised me you'd paint the kitchen ... the dining room chairs need to be varnished

Harold sighed even heavier.

and the carpet in the living room needs to be—

"Mildred, I just want to watch my TV shows. I'm eighty-two years old. I just want to watch TV. I don't need to paint the kitchen. I don't even use the dining room anymore."

but Harold

"It's only a house. Wood, plaster, and stone. Fifty years from now—hell, ten years from now—it won't matter one iota if I've painted the kitchen or not. If the house hasn't been bulldozed, it will be owned by someone else who will likely repaint and remodel everything anyway. Those green drapes you spent days deciding on? The next owner will rip them down and put up purple ones. It's just a house, Mildred. I refuse to waste what little time I have left in life toiling over a house."

He wasn't quite sure, but he thought he then heard Mildred crying. Can ghosts cry? If they could talk, Harold assumed they could cry.

it's our home

He nodded, and then frowned. Can you hurt a ghost's feelings?

"Yes, it *was* our home, and we kept it well. It was a beautiful, loving home" he said. His voice was calm, soothing. "And, when you lived here, I did things around the home to make you happy. I always wanted to make you happy, Mildred. But doing those things did not make me happy in the same way they did you. Do you understand? Now that you're not here, I don't care about those things. When you were here, it was our home. Now, it is my house, and I have no desire to paint anything. It is only a house. It is a home when someone lives in it. When I'm gone, none of this will matter."

paint the kitchen

Harold shook his head. He removed his hearing aids, placed them on the coffee table, and promptly fell asleep in the recliner.

* * *

"I'm sorry, Mr. Mayfield, but our technicians have tested your units and have found no malfunction. In fact, they pass every standard test with flying colors."

"Flying colors, my ass! Did you actually *listen* to them?"

"We could not duplicate what you described. Static, you said?"

"Irritating static." Harold nodded.

"Hmm … well, here's the situation, Mr. Mayfield," the twenty-something salesman behind the counter said. "The company will not allow me to replace fully functional devices. The warranty clearly states—"

"To hell with the warranty. I want new hearing aids!"

"Dad, don't be so rude to the young man," William said. "He's only trying to help."

"I can order a new pair, no problem," the salesman said. "But your insurance will not pay for a new set, and your Medicare doesn't cover it at all. You would have to pay out-of-pocket for the new hearing aids."

Harold sighed. "Fine. I just can't wear those anymore. The incessant noise will drive me insane."

"I'll cover the costs," William said to the salesman. "Do you need a down-payment?"

* * *

The new, sleek hearing aids only made Mildred's voice more distinct and shriller.

why must you be such a slob

Harold ignored her. It was becoming more difficult for him every day to do so. But, to hear the television, he also had to hear her. He had no options.

He flipped through the channels using the TV remote.

when was the last time you washed those windows

He then happened upon a show about ghost hunting, on that science fiction channel that he usually avoided. He stopped scrolling. He was never interested in these shows before, believing them to be bunk—just a bunch of supposed researchers wandering through spooky houses with flashlights and other contraptions. But now he had a different perspective. He settled back to watch the show.

* * *

"Billy, I was watching one of those ghost-chasing shows last week. Do you ever watch those shows?"

"You shouldn't watch that junk, Dad. It's all fake. There's no such thing as a ghost."

don't tell William about me

"Well, on this show, the guys looking for ghosts were using all kinds of gizmos—video cams, gadgets that could detect electromagnetic fields, and recorders that could pick up sounds and voices that the ghost chasers couldn't hear with the naked ear. They could record voices of spirits, Billy."

"Really, Dad. It's garbage."

"They're called EVPs. Electronic voice phenomena."

"It's not real. They're probably just recording fragments of radio broadcasts or CB radios or something."

"I don't know, Billy. It seemed legit to me."

"Dad—"

"I think I'm picking up EVPs through my hearing aids."

William stared at his father.

"Your mother has been talking to me, Billy."

"Oh, Dad—"

I told you not to tell him ... I told you

* * *

"Where's the friggin' remote?" Harold said aloud to the others in the room. No one seemed to hear him, which didn't surprise him in the least. He'd been largely ignored at the Shady Oaks Retirement Home, ever since Billy had left him here the week before.

will you stop worrying about the stupid television

Harold sat on the couch in the TV room, facing the big-screen television fastened high on the wall.

why did you let William put you in this place

The remote wasn't on the coffee table in front of him, just a pile of old magazines. The end table nearest him was piled with hardback books—no remote.

is William selling our house

"Yes, Mildred, Billy is selling our house. Do you see the remote anywhere?"

you can't let William sell the house

"Sure I can. I'm no longer living there. And you're no longer living."

why are you being so cruel

"Just stating the obvious. So, do you see the remote or not?"

don't you care about our home

"Fine. Don't help me then."

A large woman slept at the other end of the couch, her head tilted back, drool pooling at the corner of her mouth. Her snoring was cavernous. The remote was buried between her clenched thighs.

"Dammit," Harold said. He reached for the remote, careful not to touch the woman and wake her.

you need to get on the phone immediately and call William

Harold gingerly extricated the remote. It was slathered with the woman's thigh sweat. "Dammit," he said again.

call William and tell him not to sell our house ... call him now

He started flipping through the channels, trying to find anything of interest. Anything to take his mind away.

I want you to move back into our house and ... and ... fix things

There was an episode of *Matlock*. Thank the stars and all that is holy! He cranked up the volume on the TV.

Harold, are you listening to me

He closed his eyes. It was time. Long past time.

don't ignore me

He twisted the hearing aid from his left ear, rolled it in his palm, contemplating …

Harold, don't you dare

… and then dropped the tiny device to the floor. He crushed it under his heel like a walnut.

"I love you, Mildred," he whispered.

He reached for the hearing aid in his right ear …

NOOOOOOOO

… dropped it to the floor and crushed it as well.

The silence was immediate, welcome relief.

Harold looked around the room at his fellow Shady Oaks denizens, all in varied degrees of conversation. A group of old codgers played poker at a card table in the corner—maybe he'd join them tomorrow night. He glanced at the sleeping woman slouched on the couch next to him. No one seemed to have noticed his actions. He reached down to the floor and gathered the debris in his hand, and then placed the ruined hearing aids in his shirt pocket. He'd flush them down the toilet when he returned to his room later in the evening.

Harold stared for a time at the television, hearing nothing but a low growl, even with the TV at full volume. The episode of *Matlock* was one he'd seen so many times that he didn't have to hear the TV to know what Andy Griffith was saying.

He abruptly realized just how boring television reruns were.

Harold sighed. What now? Thumb twiddling?

Then, he remembered the pile of books stacked on the end table, all hardbacks. The book on the top of the pile was Mickey Spillane's classic *I, the Jury*.

Why had he never read any books by Mickey Spillane? Or Dashiell Hammett? Or Raymond Chandler? Or Ed McBain? Or any number of other crime and mystery novelists? He always meant to read the classics but had never gotten around to it. Shady Oaks had a large library downstairs, just waiting for exploration.

He picked up the Spillane book. With a smile, he opened it, turned to the first page.

And began to read.

JASON TRIES ONLINE DATING

"So, I see from your profile that you enjoy camping and long walks in the woods." Jennifer Ohrbach looked up at him from across the table. She'd been stabbing at her salad with a fork, but not eating much, just pushing the greens around on the plate.

"I'm an outdoorsy kinda guy," Jason said. He could see the carotids pulsing in her slim neck.

"Crystal Lake? Isn't that a campground or something?"

"It's upstate. Nice, tranquil place. Well, most of the time. Sometimes the screaming gets to you."

"Lots of kids, huh?"

Jason nodded. "One of my favorite places, ever since I was a boy."

"Well, you're certainly a quiet guy. I like that. I like long walks through the woods, too."

"Ahem."

"So, I take it you like hockey?"

"Huh?"

"Your profile picture."

"Oh, that. Yes, I, eh, enjoy hockey."

"I thought it was cute, that mask thing. You must have a weird sense of humor. I like that, too!"

He wondered how many guys she'd been with. Probably plenty. He'd have to rectify that.

Mom really lost her head over that last girl. She'd been so critical of all his girlfriends. Well, mostly women he'd admired from afar. His mother had been so fussy about promiscuous teenage girls. Sluts, she called them. Fornicators. Tramps. Jason thought most of them were kinda cute. Particularly after he'd finished with them.

"You've hardly eaten your dinner," Jennifer said. "Aren't you hungry? Don't you like it?"

"I've never been to this restaurant. Actually, I don't eat out very often. The steak's overdone. I prefer it a little bloodier than this, ya know?"

"So, you like it on the rare side. We can send it back."

"No, no. It's okay. I see you haven't eaten much either."

"Well, a girl has to watch her figure." She smiled. Jason liked her smile. He liked her pulsing carotids more.

"On your profile, you wrote that your profession was a butcher. At a local market?"

"Oh, I go wherever I'm needed."

"So, a traveling butcher? I've never heard of such a thing."

"I have a unique job, that's for sure."

"Would you say you're driven by your career? I like a man with a strong work ethic."

"You could say that, sure."

What's with the third degree? If there was a major drawback to online dating, it was this. All these women were looking for a husband. A date was like a job interview. His online profile was a résumé. Sheesh!

When Jason scrolled through the profiles on the dating site earlier, most of the women in the photos had no appeal to him at all. But this brunette, this Jennifer Ohrbach, jumped off the screen. He'd liked this one. She looked like she had … spunk. She had incredible blue eyes. A pleasant smile—although her lips were a little thin. But that didn't matter to him. A minor detail. Of course, her photo didn't reveal her figure, but that didn't matter either. He could imagine. And he did.

But now, sitting with her at dinner, he couldn't believe how BORING she was.

Then he realized the awkward silence between them. They'd been eating without talking for five or more minutes. He looked up from his plate at her.

She tilted her head. She smiled.

"So, do you have any questions for me?" she said.

Jason shrugged. "I don't know." Truth was, he didn't care.

"Oh, c'mon! You must have at least *one* question."

"Um … are you a fast runner?"

"You mean, like a 5K sort of thing?"

"I suppose it could be 5K, sure."

"No, I'm not much of a runner. More of a jogger. You?"

"I like slow walking. Some might even say stalking. I get where I'm going eventually, though."

"Do you work out? I enjoy going to the gym, especially for yoga. I tried CrossFit, but that was too intense for me."

"No, I don't work out. But I can certainly appreciate a flexible woman."

Jennifer blushed. "Oh, you …"

Jason then realized she was perfect. She was just irritating enough to justify his fun and games. He would enjoy her later.

"You know, you're cute," she said. "I mean, you're not much of a talker, but that's okay. I talk enough for the both of us."

You've got that right, Jason thought.

"Do you enjoy movies?" she said. "I love going to movies. Do you?"

"I've been *in* a few movies," Jason said. He ate a forkful of baked potato. It was swimming in butter and sour cream and crusted with bacon. Not bad. Certainly better than the steak.

"Really? So, you're a butcher *and* an actor?"

"Well …"

"Anything I would have seen?"

"Probably not. Do you like horror movies?"

"I prefer romantic comedies. I did see that movie with the sparkling vampire, though. What was that? Twilight?"

Oh my God, Jason thought. Could this woman be any lamer?

"No, my movies were … um … darker than that."

"Oh."

"I would be happy to show you one of my movies someday. In fact, you can be in my next one."

"Oh!"

"You might enjoy it. I know I would."

"Okay, that sounds like fun."

"It's a date then," he said. He forced a smile.

"So, you *do* want to see me again?"

They always asked this. Never fails. There was a reason they used a dating service—they were all looking for that perfect guy. That mythical guy who never existed. Sad, really. But it was a boon for him. Easy pickings.

"Of course," he said. The lie came easily to him these days. In the end, it wouldn't matter anyway. "Would you like to take a walk in the park? It's a quiet evening."

"Oooh, I'd love to!"

Jason stood and then took her hand to help her from the table. He put his arm around her shoulder.

"It's a full moon, really romantic," he said. "I'll just need to stop by my car to get my machete. You never know who you might run into out there."

- 152 -

BLUE EYE BURN

April 7, 1971

She has an American father, Joe Chance thought.

Her eyes were sapphires. Weren't many Vietnamese kids with blue eyes. The girl—five, maybe six years old—stood alone in the center of a mud path leading to her small village, a cluster of huts with rice paddies on one side and dense jungle on the other. Chance was on point, so he was the first to see her. Her smile was as bright as her incredible eyes.

"What's your name, kiddo?" he said.

She didn't answer. Just smiled up at him as if he were a newfound deity.

Chance squatted in front of her, readjusting his M-16 on his shoulder to get down to her level. He returned her smile. "My name is Joe."

She then beamed, instantly winning his heart. "G.I. Joe?" she said, tilting her head.

Chance laughed. "I guess I am, at that. What's your name, kid?"

She continued to smile, but clearly didn't understand him.

"Here, look at this." He reached into his pack and pulled out a red wooden yo-yo with a silver stripe down its center. "This is a Duncan Super Tournament Tops. Perfectly balanced. The best for doing tricks. But you have no idea what I'm saying, do you?"

He winked at her, and then stood and performed a Loop the Loop. Next came Around the World, Skin the Cat, and finally Rock the Baby. The girl was wholly mystified, as were a few of his fellow grunts who had gathered around.

Chance crouched in front of the girl again. He'd never seen such joy in anyone's eyes. "Here ya go, kid." He handed her the yo-yo.

The girl rolled the yo-yo in her hand, treating it as though it were a precious jewel. Then she turned and ran toward the village, squealing with delight.

When Chance stood, his unit commander, Lt. Anderson, was standing just behind him. "Not a good idea," Anderson said.

"Sir?"

"Don't want to get too close to the locals, Chance."

"It's just a little girl, sir."

Anderson shook his head. "Just don't be getting paternal on me. I need you on your toes, not worrying about a little girl."

"No problem," Chance said.

November 3, 2002

The stench of napalm made Chance bolt upright in his bed, sweat-drenched and shivering.

It was the same dream, always the same dream. In it, he reaches down to the girl, her entire body engulfed in liquid fire. As his hands touch her, the devouring flames race up his arms toward his face. Chance always awoke before the fire reached his eyes. Yet, even once awake, the acrid smell of napalm and the sick-sweet odor of scorched flesh clawed at his nostrils and clung to the back of his throat.

He closed his eyes, forcing the images from his mind with happier memories of his childhood, a technique he learned in therapy. He'd been through counseling at the VA hospital off and on for three decades, but nothing eliminated the persistent nightmare. More recently, he'd been seeing the girl during his waking hours—a glimpse of her playing on the playground at an inner-city Catholic school, on a bus passing his car as he drove to work on I-95, even once at the local supermarket. A trick of light, a ghost, a phantom of memory? He could no longer be sure.

Chance sensed that he was not alone in the dark bedroom. He turned his head in time to see a small figure receding into the shadows of the corner.

I never knew your name, he thought.

He thrust his hand toward the bedstand, dangerously close to knocking the lamp to the floor. His trembling fingers found the switch, and then light flooded the room.

The bedroom corner was empty, as he expected. Just his imagination, a remnant of the dream.

Only this time there was a charred Duncan yo-yo at the foot of his bed.

November 5, 2002

"Do you believe in ghosts, Dr. Baxter?"

The psychiatrist didn't even look up from his notepad as he answered. "I believe what you experienced was merely an extension of your recurrent nightmare. Like the yo-yo on your bed ..."

"Yes?"

"... that disappeared before your eyes. Like the girl who faded into the shadows. All illusion. Only residual elements of your dream."

Chance realized Baxter had not answered his question, but he decided not to pursue it. He stared at the doctor on the other side of the imposing desk. No comfortable therapy couch here. Dr. Baxter had his own style of treatment that was coldly appropriate for a VA hospital.

Then Chance heard the distinct whir of a yo-yo. He resisted the urge to turn in his chair, for he knew what was behind him. Baxter had a framed photo of his wife on the desk and, in the glass's reflection, Chance could see the girl just past his right shoulder, playing with a red yo-yo.

"You managed three years without a reported hallucinatory episode," Baxter said, finally looking up at him.

"That's right." *That's all I've reported*, Chance thought.

"Why now? What do you think triggered the renewed nightmares?"

The whir of a yo-yo.

"Any thoughts?" Dr. Baxter prodded.

"I think it's about 911. Iraq. Afghanistan. All that."

"How so?"

"It's Vietnam again." *Tell the good doctor what he wanted to hear.* Chance could still see the girl's reflection. Why couldn't Baxter see her?

Baxter nodded. "And so now you see the girl again."

"Yes."

The whir of a yo-yo.

"I think we'll prescribe Xanax for you. Just an antidepressant to help you sleep. That helped before, didn't it?"

"Yes, I believe so. Thank you."

"Just wondering," Baxter said. "In these dreams, these hallucinations. Have you ever confronted the girl? Ever actually talked with her?"

The whir of a yo-yo.

"No, I don't believe I have."

Chance then turned in his chair.

The girl was not there.

April 10, 1971

Chance's unit had been using the village as a reconnaissance point for three days when the firestorm came. Stationed in Da Nang, his unit had been deployed to the Quang Tri province to recon Charlie positions in questionable villages just south of the DMZ. The Vietcong infested the jungles like roaches.

Late that afternoon, Chance stood with a group of soldiers just outside the village when they heard a Claymore antipersonnel mine explode to the south. Semi-automatic fire started soon after, and the soldiers scrambled for cover. Charlie was on the move.

Two B-57s roared low over the jungle, releasing napalm in parallel lines. But the pilots must have misjudged the wind, for much of the incendiary jelly splattered on the tiny cluster of huts. The screaming began.

The blue-eyed girl came shrieking from the jungle, a human torch drenched with napalm. Despite the surrounding chaos, Chance rushed toward her. She was naked, her clothes already burned from her body. She fell into the mud and started to roll frantically, attempting to extinguish the flames. By the time Chance reached her, mud covered her, but the white phosphorus in the napalm continued to dissolve her flesh. Her unearthly wail drilled into his head. As he reached down to her, someone grabbed his shoulders and pulled him back.

"Charlie's infiltrated the perimeter," Anderson said. "We gotta move!"

"Not without her."

Anderson glanced down at the girl writing in the mud and then looked Chance square in the eyes. "She's a goner, man. The whole village is toast."

"She needs a medic. We can save her."

"We gotta move, Joe. No medic is going to fly in here with the VC clobbering the back door. We can't help her."

"We have to."

"We can't," Anderson said. "Look, I told you not to get close, man. I *told* you."

A mortar exploded on the other side of the village, on;y fifty yards away. More gunfire. More screaming.

"I'm not leaving her here for the VC to find," Chance said.

Anderson sighed, nodded. "Okay, okay. Then you gotta do what you gotta do." He slapped Chance on the shoulder. "Just don't take long. Charlie is pissing down our necks."

Anderson joined the other soldiers rushing out of the village.

Chance looked down at the girl. Her eyes were wide with agony and utter horror.

"I'm so sorry, kiddo," he whispered. "So sorry you were born in this hellhole."

He did what he had to do.

November 15, 2002

Chance stood in the shower, his head upturned to catch the icy blast of water full on his face. His eyes were closed. After a long day on the line at Chrysler, punching the same bolt into the same hole for twelve hours, he felt completely exhausted. He needed the overtime, but he also needed the sleep.

In his peripheral vision, he saw a small figure standing just outside the shower stall, her silhouette on the shower curtain. He turned off the faucet and then wiped the water from his eyes. He stared at the tiled wall, not wanting to turn, not wanting to confront her.

"Why are you here?" he whispered.

She didn't answer.

Silence.

"What do you want?" he asked, louder this time.

She didn't move.

Chance remained silent and motionless for what seemed an eternity, but was only a few seconds. He then placed his hand on the shower curtain and gently pulled it aside.

The girl looked exactly like the five-year-old he remembered, her blue eyes wide and unblinking. There was a deep sadness in her features, however, her eyes rimmed with red, as if she'd been crying.

He dropped to his knees on the shower floor and, putting his face in his hands, sobbed. "I'm sorry, so sorry," he cried. "You must know I'm sorry for what happened to you that day. Please tell me you forgive me. Please tell me."

Her hand fell on his shoulder. He felt it. It was real. But the touch was also weightless, ephemeral. He looked up at her.

"Oh, G.I. Joe," she said. Her voice was mature, as if she had aged over the years as he had.

She smiled now, and he was immediately back in the jungle thirty years ago, looking into those same incredible blue eyes as he crouched in front of her. He returned her smile, as he had done so many years before. He suddenly realized she wasn't a ghost at all. She was an angel.

"I forgave you long ago," she said. "It's time to forgive yourself."

As her words worked into his mind, she started to fade, to dissolve before his eyes. "No, wait—"

Then she was gone. He was alone, squatting naked on his shower floor.

December 23, 2002

Chance was Santa Claus in front of a supermarket, ringing a bell and watching families and other last-minute shoppers hustle and bustle around him, most of them dropping change and often bills into his red kettle as they passed. In two days, he would be having Christmas dinner at his sister's house in Baltimore. He looked forward to exchanging gifts with her family, the only family he had left.

He had cancelled his last appointment with Dr. Baxter earlier in the month, stopped taking the Xanax. He had no need for either anymore.

A large group of carolers joined him on the sidewalk, and he sang "Angels We Have Heard on High" with them. A tiny face with sapphire eyes briefly appeared in the crowd. He only saw her for a second, and then she was gone.

He smiled. He rang the bell.

THE CONWRIGHT TRILOGY

WELCOME TO THE FOOD CHAIN

"Flash, huh?" The fat man leveled his eyes at the slender man sitting across the table from him. "Why do they call you Flash? Like that comic book guy in the red tights?"

"Something like that. I don't like to waste time," Conwright said. "I was a high school track star. Got the nickname back then. That was in another life, a distant time."

The fat man, Albert Nigroponte, nodded, grabbed another crab from the table. He ate a prodigious amount of steamed crabs and drank his Pabst Blue Ribbon by the keg. His appetite and obsession had impelled him, over the years, to purchase three "all-you-can-eat" seafood joints on the shores of the Chesapeake Bay. The largest and most profitable restaurant, The Magnificent Wharf, was in Annapolis. The restaurant in St. Michael's, The Amber Whale, was the swankiest, for the tourists. The establishment in Havre de Grace, The Hammer & Claw, was a true dive. Nigroponte had chosen the H&C to meet

Conwright to arrange their business.

At Nigroponte's request, Conwright entered the restaurant after hours, long after the restaurant staff had departed for the evening. Nigroponte sat alone at a corner table covered with newspaper. Piled on the newspaper were at least three dozen fiery red, steamed blue crabs. Nigroponte feasted like Neptune. The restaurant reeked of Old Bay seasoning and a distinct, stagnant wharf odor, a foul blend of rotting fish entrails and brine.

"So, can you do the job?"

"In my sleep," Conwright said. "For the right price."

"How much?"

"Fifty thousand."

Nigroponte grumbled and shook his head. "No friggin' way. She ain't worth that. No way."

"No, she's not. But I am. This is a business. I'm a businessman. My reputation speaks for itself or I wouldn't be here. I give you a discount, every slob and his brother wants a discount. My reputation suffers."

"Screw your reputation." Nigroponte pointed an amputated crab claw at him. "I ain't payin' no fifty grand for that bimbo."

Conwright got up from the table.

"Wait a minute! Just one friggin' minute." Nigroponte pasted on a chummy, let's-be-pals smile. "Ya gotta work with me on this. Cut me a break, okay?"

"Yeah, sure. You own the whole marina. That's your yacht in the slip right outside this window. And you can't afford fifty thousand? Cut *me* a break."

"Listen, I have this cash flow problem, ya see. No thanks to that bloodsuckin' bitch, let me tell ya. Bleedin' me friggin' dry."

"No offense, but I don't need the sob story. Do you want me to off her or not?"

"Yeah. And don't leave nothin' for the medical examiner."

"I'll do it right, don't worry. But I don't come cheap. Take it or leave it."

Nigroponte smashed a crab claw with a wooden mallet, and then carefully removed the lump of blushing white meat from the split shell. He eyed Conwright, no longer smiling.

"You're one hardass, ain't ya, Conwright? Think you've got the world by the cojones."

Conwright sighed. "You get what you pay for, Mr. Nigroponte."

The fat man grunted. "Twenty-five thousand."

Conwright shook his head. "Fifty thousand, and there's no way they can link it to you. They won't even find the body."

"Thirty thousand. That's my top dollar."

"Fifty thousand. And that's a bargain."

"Screw you." Nigroponte pounded another crab claw with his mallet. "I'll find some other schmuck to do her. A derelict on the street would do it for a bottle of cheap gin."

"And you'd be in jail the next day. Up to you."

Nigroponte popped another morsel of crab into his mouth and washed it down with some Pabst. "I'm not puttin' up more than thirty thousand," he said. He looked into Conwright's eyes as he spoke. "It's a dog-eat-dog world, Flash. Welcome to the friggin' food chain, ya know? I didn't get here on my good looks or blind luck. Like you, I've done my homework. My contacts, our mutual acquaintances, told me how to deal with you. I know ya need the cash. I know ya owe Solomon Ventura a sizeable chunk of change. You're in no position to negotiate."

When Conwright frowned at the mention of Ventura, Nigroponte knew he had him. After a bad run of luck in Atlantic City last week, Conwright was in for twenty Gs—plus interest, of course—with Solly Ventura. Nigroponte knew of Solly from his early days in South Philly, where he still had contacts. Solly was *not* someone you'd want to screw over.

"You trust these people, these contacts of yours?" Conwright asked.

"I trust them. They recommended you highly."

Conwright stared at the fat man, still frowning. Nigroponte cracked open another crab claw, waiting. The silence seemed impenetrable.

"Okay," Conwright finally said, pasting on his own best let's-be-pals smile. "Deal. But I have expenses. I need ten thousand up front, twenty thousand when the job's done."

Nigroponte smiled like a cat with a mouse under its paw. "Done," he said. He pulled a wad of bills from somewhere in the folds of his pants and peeled off the cash, six Gs and the rest in C notes—petty cash to the fat man. When Conwright took the money, the bills were damp with Nigroponte's perspiration.

"I need a week, maybe more, to figure out her routines

and determine when best to take her out and in what manner. I'll meet you here a week from today to finalize our arrangement."

Nigroponte nodded. "Same time is fine, but I don't like talkin' here. Never know who might walk in, particularly Sheila. Meet me on the Barnacled Dolphin." He pointed out the window to his yacht. "We'll go out on the bay, more privacy."

"That would be ideal."

For the next hour, Nigroponte told Conwright everything he knew about Sheila's typical day, her favorite haunts, and her friends.

* * *

With all the young Navy recruits in Annapolis, Sheila Nigroponte thought it was "strategic" to relocate here after her separation from her toady husband. She was an attractive, tall redhead with manufactured breasts, collagen-pumped lips, and a well-sculpted nose. Why not make the best of her investments? She had no shortage of boyfriends. She still managed The Magnificent Wharf on the waterfront, as she had during her brief marriage, but now only in a cursory manner. Hers was a social life.

Her only true routine was a daily workout at Gold's Gym, only a few blocks from where she lived, from four to five o'clock. Dinner followed this at one of the many restaurants in the area, usually with a different man every night. She ate at The Magnificent Wharf on Friday evenings. When the crowd hummed, she would flit from table to table talking with prominent local socialites. Her marriage to Nigroponte provided access to a massive bank account and was certainly a step up the social ladder for her, but little else.

Sheila took pride in being a "cougar"—she was always on the prowl for fresh meat. She'd noticed the new guy at the gym last week. Not a meathead with bulging muscles, he was quite slender and well-toned—probably a cyclist or a runner, from the build. Not bad-looking either, but not Brad Pitt by a long shot. Still, attractive enough. She watched him from afar for a few days. He seemed to be a loner, not interacting often with the other gym patrons.

He was working out on a weight bench when she finally approached him. Sheila stood next to the bench, watching him pump the barbells. When he noticed her, she smiled.

"Hi," he said, returning her smile.

"Need someone to spot you?"

"Nah, but thanks for asking. I'm used to working out alone."

"You new in town?" she purred.

He sat up on the bench and threw a towel over his shoulder. "Just a few weeks. I'm originally from South Jersey."

"I noticed you last Friday and thought I'd introduce myself. I'm Sheila Nigroponte." She moved closer to offer him a better view of her cleavage.

"I'm Jeremy," he said. "Jeremy Irons."

"Like the British actor?"

"A favorite of my mother's, yes."

Sheila wondered if she was older than his mother. No matter.

"Finding your way around town okay?"

"Pretty much. I don't know anyone here. My boss sent me here to open a new satellite office, so I'm pretty much on my own. Just me and an empty office right now."

"What do you do?"

"Asian imports, mostly from India. I know, I know! In Annapolis? I guess my boss knows what he's doing." He smiled at her again. "I'm looking for a good seafood restaurant, a place that knows how to cook mahi-mahi. You'd think in Annapolis I'd be able to find something. Got any suggestions?"

"I certainly do. The Magnificent Wharf." Her smile broadened. "Are you asking me to dinner?"

"Depends. Are you going to say yes?"

"If you're paying."

"My pleasure."

No, mine, Sheila thought.

* * *

Nigroponte had been drinking before they left the dock in Havre de Grace at the mouth of the Susquehanna. Conwright had to trust his navigational skills, that he could handle the Barnacled Dolphin on a moonlit night.

A large, lidded pot of steamed crabs waited on deck. Once they'd anchored in the bay, Nigroponte planned to feast again. He already had a table covered with newspaper and assorted mallets, nutcrackers, and skewers ready to fulfill the task. Conwright lifted the lid and looked into the pot.

"Know much about crabs?" Nigroponte asked.

"Not really."

"Nasty little scavengers. They make dead things disappear. They serve their purpose. Kinda like you, huh, Flash? Make dead things disappear?"

Conwright shrugged. "I'm allergic to shellfish."

"Too bad. A keg and a few dozen crabs and I'm a happy man. Didja ever steam crabs, Conwright? Ya throw them in the pot alive, put the lid on, then turn up the heat. Get the steam rollin'. Listen to 'em scramble to get away from the heat. Too bad they can't scream. Can ya imagine being slowly steamed to death?"

"No, I suppose not." But Conwright *could* imagine steaming someone to death, the flesh bubbling and melting. He could easily picture this in his head and imagined Sheila screaming as she melted to goo.

Conwright loved his work. It was the planning, the fantasizing, the playing out of death scenarios that made it fun and worthwhile—the "hit" was often frustratingly mundane. Reality never lived up to his fantasies. It was always better to go for the clean kill, leaving nothing for the CSI folks, than to actually realize what he could imagine.

Killing for fun—as in his earlier, formative days—had been satisfying.

Killing for *pay* was even more so, even if he had to sacrifice creativity occasionally.

He could easily imagine killing Sheila Nigroponte using

a great variety of entertaining methods. She was a vain woman who treasured her well-styled auburn hair. He would definitely shave her head first. That led him to think of an electric chair, and he wondered if electrocution was an option. Probably not, but it would be fun to watch her fry. So many ways to kill her; he could have fun with her.

Nigroponte anchored the Barnacled Dolphin off the southern tip of Kent Island. Conwright could see the lights of Annapolis to the northwest. There were a few boats to the far south, probably crabbers pulling up their pots.

Conwright joined Nigroponte in the cabin. The fat man retrieved two beers from the fridge, handing one to Conwright.

"So, have ya decided how you're going to do it?"

"The way I normally do it, simple and fast."

"Where?"

"I've been seeing her at the gym, gaining her trust, so to speak."

"Good, good."

"We're going out to dinner this Friday night. When I'm alone with her and the time is right ..."

"Excellent!"

"She won't suspect a thing. She'll be in the middle of a conversation with me when I slip the gun out. Sheila won't realize anything until it's too late. It'll happen so fast, she won't feel a thing. Maybe there'll be a look of surprise on her face, but more likely a look of indifference. That's the normal reaction. I always look them in the eye. Sometimes you can see the soul depart from the body, like a vapor."

Nigroponte stared at him like he was a nutcase. "Yeah,

yeah. Whatever. As long as ya do it, that's all I care. And don't look for her soul, 'cause she ain't got one."

When they got to the deck, Nigroponte went straight to the pot of crabs. He was already drunk.

"Do ya really think you have her fooled?" he asked as he took the lid off the pot. "She's not stupid, ya know. She could be on to ya, settin' you up for somethin' nasty." He reached into the pot and started yanking out crabs and throwing them on the table.

"She trusts me. She wouldn't turn on me now."

Nigroponte chuckled. "You don't know my wife."

"Oh, I know your wife."

Conwright pulled his Bernadelli, a palm-size Italian .22 automatic, from the holster hidden under his left arm. He loved the slick, warm metal feel of it in his hand. It fit so perfectly in his fingers.

As Nigroponte turned toward him, Conwright looked him straight in the eye. He lifted the gun and pulled the trigger once in a practiced, fluid motion. The bullet perforated Nigroponte's forehead just above his left eye. The single .22 slug ricocheted within his skull like a pinball razor, shredding brain tissue and vital blood vessels. When Conwright could get close enough to his target, the .22 was his favorite means of execution. When Nigroponte's body tumbled to the deck, he stood over him and put another slug in his head, just to be sure.

"I know your wife," Conwright repeated. "And she pays a hell of a lot better than you do."

He put the lid back on the pot of crabs. No feasting tonight.

Conwright turned off all the lights on the yacht, save for one below deck. Then he went back to Nigroponte's corpse. He had to get the wedding band off his bloated finger. No wonder Sheila wanted that as evidence that he'd completed the job—she knew he'd have to cut off the finger to get the ring. He couldn't get the ring past the first knuckle. He found a filet knife in a tackle box in the cabin and used that to peel the flesh from the bone. Conwright tossed the bloody pulp off the yacht. With Nigroponte's finger stripped to the bone, he had no trouble removing the ring.

Conwright pulled up the anchor and cut the rope. Using the rope, he lashed Nigroponte's bulk to the anchor, and then, with great effort, tipped him over the side. The fat man went to the bottom like a cannonball.

As he watched Nigroponte disappear into the dark water, he wondered how long it would take the crabs to find the decaying corpse. *Welcome to the food chain, Nigroponte.* He suspected the crabs would come in with the tide and quickly discover the smorgasbord resting on the bottom of the bay. Conwright closed his eyes, imagining hundreds of crabs feasting on the rotting bulk. The larger crabs would come first for the soft tissues of Nigroponte's gaping mouth and tongue. Several crabs might wriggle down his throat for the sweeter meat. In time, the smaller crustaceans would eventually find their way into other orifices, gaining access to the brain. Ah, there was the real prize! The constant pull and tug of their mandibles and claws would come to bear on the tougher optic nerves and muscles. Nigroponte's eyes would twitch and turn beneath the closed eyelids, giving the corpse the illusion of REM sleep. The eyes would finally collapse into the sockets as the crabs feast from within. Conwright opened his eyes, looked up at the moon.

Nah, probably couldn't happen that way.

He sighed, turned away from the water.

He then steered the yacht toward the mouth of the Chesapeake. Once on the Atlantic, he headed north up the coast to Cape May. He'd already contacted Solly Ventura the night before, who'd agreed to take the yacht in payment for the gambling debt Conwright owed him.

* * *

On Friday night, the Magnificent Wharf buzzed with crowds on Friday night when Sheila and Conwright met for their final transaction. She'd already ordered dinner before he arrived. He had no intention of staying. She did not know this.

Many men—indeed, most—would find Sheila alluring and irresistible. Albert Nigroponte certainly did, much to his misfortune. But Conwright knew her black heart, knew the ugliness inside. He'd known women like her throughout his life—probably went with the trade, he figured. Femmes fatales. He felt no attraction whatsoever to the recently widowed Mrs. Nigroponte.

"No thanks," he said, responding to her proposal. "I'm sure an evening with you would indeed be pleasurable, in an animal way. But I'm only here for the money."

Her smile instantly dissolved, and something darkened in her eyes. He'd seen it a hundred times before.

"Figures," she said with disgust. "You men are all alike. Where's the ring?"

Conwright pulled the wedding band from his shirt pocket and slid it across the table to her.

She picked it up and examined it. "How did you get it off his finger?"

"The hard way."

"I bet." Her grin was the definition of malice.

She pushed the manila envelope across the table to him—fifty thousand in laundered hundred-dollar bills. "I suppose you want to count it?"

"No, I trust you." If she'd shortchanged him, Conwright could find her. In that circumstance, she would not want to see him again. He imagined her sitting across the table from him with a shaved head. He imagined a car battery, jumper cables, and damp sponges, just to get the party started. Maybe, even if she didn't stiff him, he'd come back for a visit, for a bonus round with her. The fat man paid him ten Gs, after all—not the full contract, but enough. Conwright smiled.

A young waiter stepped up to the table with a tray. "Crab Imperial?" he asked, looking back and forth between the two.

"Here," she said.

After placing the plate before Sheila, the waiter turned to Conwright.

"Would you like to order now, sir?"

"No, no. I was just leaving."

"The Crab Imperial is superb, sir," the waiter continued. "Sweet lump crab, fresh from the bay this morning."

"No thanks," Conwright said. "I'm allergic to shellfish."

RIGHT-HAND MAN

The two remaining crème donuts were as hard as a bull's ass, and the coffee was this side of motor oil. It was time to make another run to Dunkin' Donuts—as soon as it got dark and he could slip out unnoticed. The donut joint had a restroom and a payphone. The restroom was a godsend.

He hated to recon his targets.

Francis "Flash" Conwright sat at a second-floor window of a dark, vacant house, holding high-powered binoculars to his eyes with one hand and a cell phone to his ear with the other. It was a burner phone, and he had no intention of staying on it long. He watched another seemingly empty house across the street, five doors down.

"I don't know. Something doesn't smell right."

"What's the problem?" Solly Ventura asked.

"Intuition, I guess. I can't put my finger on it, but something doesn't add up. I have to trust my intuition with these things. Saved my ass more than once." Conwright sighed. "I'm getting too old for this shit, Solly."

"What are you talking about? You're only forty-two and in the best shape of your life!"

"I'm eating donuts and crap food and drinking coffee by the friggin' gallon. I haven't worked out in weeks."

"So? You're sweating your ass off and probably smell like a syphilitic Tijuana whore. You're bored beyond belief sitting in that room. I know it's the least favorite part of your job, but it's a necessary evil. You know that. How long now?"

"Three days. You're right. I'd kill for a shower. It's so hot in here, I've got perpetual swamp-ass. I'm dying to get this over with, just to get reacquainted with air-conditioning."

"Look, don't start doubting yourself. You're the best in the business—"

"—and getting older—"

"I don't want to hear that shit. You've got years yet. Hell, you're at your prime. Listen to me. Don't doubt yourself."

"I hear you, Solly," Conwright said. But he had plenty of doubt. He never ate tons of junk food during other stakeouts. Something had changed. He had changed. Was he getting soft? "Listen, let me call you back in about an hour."

Conwright ended the call and pocketed the phone; he'd toss it down a storm drain later. He watched the tall man standing guard on the lawn in front of his target house. The guy obviously didn't care if he was conspicuous or not. But why would he care? The entire development was under construction, and there were no residents. The perfect sanctuary for a mobster in hiding. Conwright didn't recognize the thug, but he knew the old man, Cartanza, was in the house.

Vito Cartanza had been an enforcer in the Jersey mob most of his life, moving up in the ranks until, at eighty, he finally found religion and turned state's evidence. The Jersey families didn't take kindly to this and had already attempted twice to take out Cartanza. The feds offered to put Cartanza into witness protection, but the old man didn't want to go into protective custody. Instead, he fled New Jersey with four of his henchmen, ending up in a house in a new real estate development in Paradise, PA, just outside Lancaster. Amish country. Rolling farmland. Horses and buggies. A slower lifestyle.

What was bothering him? Not like he hadn't faced similar scenarios in the past. He already knew the layout of the house from building plans. Had scoped out the neighborhood, knew the ins and outs of the construction crews now building houses on the far side of the development. No obvious obstructions other than the four men protecting Cartanza. Challenging, but not problematic.

When the sun went down, he slipped out of the back of the empty house.

* * *

"Are you sure the old man's there?"

"I saw them bring him in two days ago," Conwright said. "Four goons and the geezer. Two guys at a time guarding the house, front and back, working shifts. Cartanza's got to be there."

Conwright took another bite from the chocolate-covered donut, cradling the payphone receiver against his shoulder. He stood in front of the donut shop, watching the darkened, vacant parking lot. Not many folks buy donuts at eleven o'clock on a hot, steamy July night.

"So, what do you want to do?" Solly asked. "You can bail at any time, no hard feelings. Or I can renegotiate the contract more to your liking if that changes anything."

Solomon Ventura was Conwright's liaison with the mob, had known him since their early days in South Philly. Whenever the Philly mafia needed a clean hit with no family ties, Solly made the arrangements with Conwright. Solly had ties with the right people in Jersey, as well. The politics of the Cartanza situation, dealing with the Jersey mob, required a special tack—precisely the situation for which Conwright was most suitable. The Philly boys wanted nothing to do with it, of course.

"I'll need to take out the four guards to get to the old man," Conwright said. "What can you do for me?"

"Financially?"

"Yes."

"I can swing five Gs a head, on top of the hundred Gs for Cartanza. I think the Jersey guys would go for that."

"What else can you do for me?"

"How so?"

"Can you tell me anything about these goombahs?" Conwright asked. "I don't know all the Jersey boys."

"Describe them."

"The one guy chain-smokes. Tall guy, probably the most observant of the bunch, seems to be perpetually on edge. Kinda bald, big ears. Lots of tats on his arms and going up his neck. Doesn't seem to talk much with the others. But also seems to be the one giving all the orders."

"Sounds like Benito Arturo."

"Benny the Artist. Heard of him. Real sleazebag."

"I'm surprised he's there. Benny doesn't go for the bodyguard thing. He must owe Cartanza big time."

"Advice?"

"I'd take him out first, if possible. He's pretty badass. You don't want to get anywhere near him. He'll rip off your arms and beat you to death with them."

"OK. There's a short guy, kinda overweight. Looks like he'd rather be somewhere else, like he could fall asleep at a moment's notice. Dark goatee, nose like a warthog. Older than the others."

"That's gotta be Louie Barcola. He's been with Cartanza for decades, an old friend. He's slow and not that bright. Shouldn't present any problems for you, though."

"A thug, built like a brick shithouse, arms wider than his head. I haven't seen much of him. Light hair, kinda long. Constantly combs it. Probably spends a lot of time in front of a mirror."

"Hmm ... could be Nicky Suffo. He used to be a boxer, and the mob owned him. If it's him, he's been breaking legs and smashing kneecaps for the past few years. Younger guy?"

"Probably early thirties."

"That's Suffo. He can kill you with one punch, so don't get within arm's length. Suffo is kind of a younger version of Cartanza, started as a mob grunt but with higher ambitions. Not sure why he would side with Cartanza unless he respects the codger. What's the fourth guy look like?"

"Rarely comes out of the house. Every time I've seen him, he's been right next to the old man. Doesn't look like mob material. Relative maybe?"

"How old is this guy?"

"Mid-twenties, maybe."

"Nah, Cartanza's kids are in their fifties," Solly said. "Describe this guy."

"Light hair, clean face. Not a goon like the other three, not the build."

"Hmmm ... sounds like Cartanza's right-hand man. Cartanza has some health issues, so maybe this guy handles the medicines, the food, and such. A nurse. Not much of a threat."

"OK, thanks, Solly. You'll check into the extra payment for the goons and let me know?"

"Sure thing. Listen, don't jump on this if you're still having doubts. Hear me? I don't want to lose my best hitter."

* * *

As soon as he entered the room, Conwright knew he was in trouble. Louie Barcola, the fat, slow one, stood opposite the door, gun raised. Stupid, stupid! How could he have let this toad get the jump on him?

"What the fuck you think you're doing here, Ace?" Barcola waved his gun toward the bedroll on the floor, the junk-food wrappers and empty coffee cups.

Conwright made a quick scan of the room. Despite the darkness, he was pretty sure he'd left nothing suspicious out in the open. The binoculars were in his back pocket. No guns were left in the room. Still, what did Barcola know?

"Look, I don't want no trouble, man," Conwright said. "I'm just squattin' here 'til somethin' turns up. I been outta work for months. My wife kicked me out. Just tryin' to get by, ya know?"

"Yet, you can afford Starbucks coffee," Barcola said, nodding to the empty cup on the floor.

Damn! He only went to Starbucks that one time.

"Look, man, I panhandle during the day, crash here at night. I know I'm trespassin', but I ain't causin' no trouble. And I don't want no trouble."

"How long you been here?"

"Coupla days. You want me to move on, I'll move on. I was lookin' to hitchhike to Philly, anyway."

Conwright started toward his bedroll as if to collect his gear, but Barcola waved his gun again, motioning him to step back.

"Maybe I'll just call the cops," Barcola said.

"Man, you don't wanna do that. Just let me go, OK?"

"Or, better still, just put a bullet in your head."

Conwright forced his voice to sound terrified. "C'mon, man, I ain't done nothin'. Just let me pack up and go. You won't see me again, swear to God." He started toward his gear again.

"Hold it there, buckaroo."

Conwright stopped, stared at the man, waiting for the next move. He still wasn't close enough. But Barcola's hesitation was promising.

"Nah, I think I'll shoot you," Barcola said, stepping forward, closer, close enough, "and worry about it later."

Conwright slapped the gun from Barcola's right hand with his left hand, striking the pressure point just above the wrist to break his grip. Simultaneously, he punched the man's left ear with his cupped right hand—a practiced maneuver that usually burst the eardrum or at least caused enough inner-ear trauma to drive an assailant to his knees. As Barcola lost his balance, Conwright yanked a length of garrote wire secreted in his sleeve, looped it around that thick neck, and used Barcola's own weight as he fell to cinch the wire around his throat. Barcola fought for breath, flailing and grasping at empty air, until, with a sharp tug,

Conwright crushed the hyoid bone, sealing the man's doom.

He dropped Barcola to the floor, uncoiled the wire from the dead man's throat, and allowed it to recoil on the spool in his sleeve. Conwright stared at the frog-eyed face, the eyes already filming. The garrote was efficient, but not enjoyable. What he could have done with a handheld circular sander and a little more time, peeling Barcola's cheeks, taking off only the top epithelial layers where the nerve endings were the keenest. Maybe even grating his porcine nose down to the cartilage. Or maybe use a filet knife and slice those meaty jowls to the bone. It would have been far more fun—and far better than the goon deserved. Conwright could have also gleaned more information about the specific layout of the house and Cartanza's defense plans—if only he'd had time to play.

Time, however, was precisely what he didn't have.

The circumstances demanded a change in strategy. The others would miss Barcola. If they had sent Barcola to the house, that meant they were probably aware of his presence. They would send someone else to investigate. Not good. He'd have to take action far earlier than expected.

Conwright pulled the binoculars from his back pocket and stepped to the window, but then hesitated. Had a glint on the binocular lens given him away? Something must have alerted them. Had they seen him come or go earlier? Or did they patrol the neighborhood and just happen to discover his gear?

Staying in the shadows, he looked out the window without the binoculars. Arturo stood on the front lawn of the home down the block, hands on hips, staring in his direction. Arturo lifted something to his ear—

—and a raking, static-filled sound came from behind Conwright, startling him. The sound came from a small device attached to Barcola's belt, a walkie-talkie of the sort often used by construction workers.

Arturo's voice, thick and venomous, came from the small speaker. "What's going on, you idiot? You've been up there for over an hour."

Conwright unclipped the device from Barcola's belt.

"Talk to me, numb-nuts!" Arturo growled.

At first, Conwright thought to mimic Barcola's voice. But he'd already made at least one stupid mistake, not securing this room. How many other dumb mistakes had he made?

"Talk to me!"

Conwright clicked the button a few times, on and off, on and off, on and off.

"Sweet Jesus, you don't even know how to work the damn thing!" Arturo said. "If you didn't find anything, get your lardass back here. Now!"

That gave Conwright some time. He hoped it was enough.

* * *

Conwright worked his way back to his car, parked just outside the development next to an abandoned gas station. The car looked like a derelict and fit in well next to the run-down garage. He was sure there were no active security cameras on the building. Popping the trunk, he pulled out the gear he thought he'd need for the job, gear that would not hamper him or slow him down if things didn't go well. He had to act fast before the other goons found Barcola's corpse.

It would be so much easier to take out Arturo and Suffo with a sniper rifle, simply by positioning himself where both guards were simultaneously in range. Of course, the gunshots would alert those in the house and make things difficult. But Conwright had never become proficient with a sniper rifle—largely because he abhorred sniper killings, much like he abhorred hunting. The thought of killing a deer from a distance—detached from the event, the deer not even aware of his presence, taking down the unsuspecting beast without even a confrontation—seemed cowardly to him. Too safe, too antiseptic. But here he faced two trained killers before he could even enter the target house. What now? He had no time to strategize as he'd hoped. He had to move before they realized they had a problem.

* * *

When construction started at the new development, sewer and water lines, electrical cables, and other utilities were the first to go in. The streets were paved, primarily through empty lots, and streetlights had been installed. There was a streetlight just past the target house, fully illuminating the front yard where Arturo now stood, smoking a cigarette. No way for a frontal attack, so Conwright worked his way to the back of the house, where he assumed Suffo was stationed.

Conwright crouched at the back of an adjoining house, scoping out the situation. From there, he could see lighting in the rear rooms, probably where Cartanza was holed up. And the flickering fluorescence of what was certainly a television. A gas-powered electric generator had been placed near the back door—Cartanza had the only electricity in the neighborhood.

Suffo stood at the back door, staring up at the moon.

Conwright heard Arturo on the walkie-talkie, trying to contact Barcola again, his voice getting louder as no response came.

"Suffo, get your ass over here!" Arturo yelled from the front yard.

Suffo grumbled, then disappeared around the end of the house. That was the break Conwright needed. He sprinted across the lot and melted into the shadows at the back of the house, working his way to the generator. He ducked behind it as Suffo returned to his position. The thug cursed under his breath, "Fuckin' Barcola. How the shit am I supposed to babysit Barcola and watch the house at the same time? Pain in my ass."

Conwright used the chugging hum of the generator to mask his movement as he approached Suffo from behind, his KA-BAR serrated knife in his right hand. Suffo became aware of him just as Conwright jammed his left hand over Suffo's mouth, tilting his head back. Before Conwright could slide the blade through Suffo's exposed throat, Suffo clenched a massive hand around Conwright's wrist, nearly breaking bone. Conwright suppressed a scream as the KA-BAR dropped to the ground. He shifted his weight, pulling harder on Suffo's head until the man's center of balance tilted him backward. Suffo still grasped Conwright's wrist, and he felt the agony of grinding bones in his hand as he, too, fell. Both men hit the ground.

Suffo was faster than Conwright expected, releasing his grip on Conwright's wrist and rolling aside, quickly bringing himself up on one knee. Conwright tried to do the same, but Suffo landed a devastating kidney punch. The pain was immediate and excruciating.

"Arturo!" Suffo yelled.

Now on his back, Conwright reached for his ankle holster, but couldn't pull up his pant leg before Suffo landed another punch straight to his stomach, driving the air from his lungs and doubling the pain in his abdomen.

"What the hell's going on?" Arturo rounded the corner of the house, gun drawn.

"This asshole tried to take me out," Suffo said. The ex-boxer stood, looking down at Conwright writhing on the ground. "You know him?"

Arturo stepped closer, gun pointed at Conwright's head. "Nope. Never seen him before."

"Just shoot him, get it over with," Suffo said.

"Can't do that, you idiot. We need to find out who he is, who sent him."

"Isn't it obvious?"

"No, it's not fuckin' obvious. We need to question him. 'Bout time we had some fun around here."

There was the crack of a gunshot, a muzzle flash at the back door of the house. Arturo staggered backward, a dark stain blossoming on his chest.

Suffo said, "What the—?" before another gunshot, a bullet this time punching a hole through the side of Suffo's head and blowing a chunk of skull the size of a lemon out the other side. Suffo tumbled to the lawn next to Conwright.

Arturo still stood, an expression of disbelief on his face as he looked down at his pulsing chest. Another shot and Arturo's head exploded; he dropped onto the grass.

Conwright looked toward the door, expecting a bullet himself. In the door's frame was the kid, the one Solly had called "the right-hand man," Cartanza's personal aide. He looked even younger than he had in the binoculars, clean-shaven and boy-band attractive. The kid held the handgun to his side, smiling at Conwright.

"So, Mr. Conwright. We finally meet. Sorry these two thugs caused you such distress."

What the hell? Conwright thought.

"May I call you Flash? Please, Flash, come into the house. Let's get acquainted." He lifted the gun. "But no funny business. I can make things very difficult for you."

* * *

Conwright's wrist throbbed, and he felt like his left kidney had exploded, judging from the pain in his lower back. How much damage had Suffo done? He could be bleeding internally, for all he knew.

He stumbled through the kitchen area, trying to maintain his balance, the kid with the gun behind him. He noticed the refrigerator, connected by a cable to the generator out back. Several cables snaked down the hall, he assumed to the living area where Cartanza now resided. He wondered if they also had running water and a functioning bathroom. Considering Cartanza's ill health and age, most likely.

"I guess you already took out Barcola, huh?" the kid asked. "I was the one who suggested he check out the house. You see, I've been expecting you."

"How?"

"How did I expect you? Simple. The man who hired me also hired you. I've known all along that you were hired to kill Cartanza. But it's not quite what you think." The kid chuckled, and that little laugh bothered Conwright the most. Why hadn't the kid put a bullet in his head? None of this made sense.

Although the rest of the house was presumably empty, the kitchen, adjoining bathroom, and dining room (now acting as a living room) were well furnished, with electrical cables running every which way. Cartanza sat in an armchair in front of a large, flat-screen TV, watching an old episode of "The A-Team." Only Cartanza was no longer capable of watching or hearing anything. His eyes bulged from his bloated, purple face; his black tongue protruded from his dark lips—a leather belt had been tightened around his throat.

"All the comforts of home, wouldn't you say?" the kid asked.

Conwright glared at him. "What's this about?"

"Like I said, I knew you were coming, knew you were here. As soon as you arrived at the house and I heard Suffo grappling with you, I took care of Cartanza. That was the plan, you see. You've been the real target all along."

"And the other two?"

"Also, in the plan, although I'd hoped you'd take them out before I had to. I must say, I'm disappointed with your performance so far. I expected more, considering your reputation."

"It's been a FUBAR day, what can I say? Are you going to tie me up, cuff me, or what?"

Then Conwright saw it—just a glint, a fraction, of fear in the kid's eyes. His captor, despite his bravado, was keeping his distance.

"Take your clothes off," the kid said.

"You're kidding."

"Not at all. I know you're carrying, and I have no intention of letting you use any of your weapons. So, take it all off."

"Just kill me now, junior. I'm not playing your games."

"No games. No games at all. Just precautions. You see, I've been paid to detain you, not kill you."

Conwright cocked his head. "What's this really about?"

"Like I said, you've been the target all along. You're a hard man to lure out into the open, Mr. Conwright. My employer has been tracking you for years. When Cartanza became a potential hit, my employer—"

"Just who is your employer?"

The kid ignored the question. "My employer hired you to take out Cartanza. What better way to draw you into the crosshairs?"

So, Conwright thought, whoever was behind this had mob connections, knew to contact Solly Ventura to contract him. Had to be someone who could fund a contract on Cartanza, someone tied to the Jersey mob—yet also someone who could hire this weasel to capture him.

"I want you nude," the kid said. "Now. Everything off. I'm not supposed to kill you, but I can put a bullet where you wouldn't want one."

Conwright sighed and undressed. He dropped his clothes in a pile next to Cartanza's chair, and then stripped off his various holsters, sheathed knives, and other killing devices (including the garrote and a pouch of shurikens). The young assassin was most impressed with Conwright's Bernadelli .22, a palm-sized handgun Conwright had positioned in a holster between his shoulder blades, easy to pull from the back of his neck—and generally missed in a pat down. The Bernadelli was Conwright's preferred firearm.

Conwright stood naked in front of the kid, arms outstretched. "Unless you want to check the crevice of my ass, that's it. Now what, junior?"

"Sit. On the floor. Legs crossed."

Conwright sat. As he did so, he glanced around the room, weighing his options. "You got a name, kid?"

"Actually, I kinda like 'The Kid.' Has an outlaw feel to it, wouldn't you say?"

"This isn't the wild west, kid. This is Amish country. We're not gunslingers."

The kid nodded. "Maybe not gunslingers, but certainly killers."

"You really don't know what you're dealing with, do you?"

The kid smiled, tipped the gun. "Inform me."

"Remember in the news, the Atlantic City Slasher, killed a dozen hookers? They never caught the guy. Or the Baltimore Strangler?"

"Man, that's old news, happened a decade or so ago. So what?" The kid's eyes narrowed. "Wait, are you——?"

"Catching on, junior."

"No way, man. A serial killer? And a hitman? BS. Pure BS." The kid laughed.

"Even hired guns take vacations. A little R and R. On the job, I don't kill unless I get paid. But on my own time, well ..."

"Bullshit!"

Conwright shrugged. "Let's just say I have unique skills and experience. For example, I can imagine attaching jumper cables to your scrotum and giving you the thrill of your short life. Plus, some fun and games with strategically placed drops of hydrochloric acid. I can hear you screaming. But that would be way too much fun. I don't mix business with pleasure, and I'm here on business. So, more than likely, I'll take the boring route and just put a bullet in your head."

The kid laughed again. "Aw, man, you're killing me here! I'm the one with the gun, dipshit. You're sitting with your nuts on the floor. Your career ends tonight, old man." He pulled a cell phone from his pants pocket, punched in a number. "Yeah, I have him here now. He's not going anywhere. No. Arturo and Suffo roughed him up a bit. I had to take them both out. Yeah, Cartanza's dead, too. No. No problem." He finished the call and then smiled at Conwright. "He'll be here soon."

"Then what?"

"Oh, I think he wants to take care of you himself. Some revenge thing. I hope it's fun to watch."

"I'm sure it will be," Conwright said. He grasped the electrical cable on the floor next to him and yanked with all his strength, sending spikes of pain from his injured kidney through his spine. The cable snapped taut against the back of the kid's ankles, toppling him backward to the floor. Conwright sprang from his sitting position, straddled his captor, and drove his flat, open hand into the kid's throat, punching the boy's larynx, causing spontaneous gagging. Conwright ripped the gun from the kid's hand, jammed the gun into the side of his knee, and fired one shot. The kid howled.

Conwright put his lips next to the kid's left ear. "What's the plan?" he asked.

The kid sobbed, his eyes wide.

"What's the friggin' plan?" Conwright repeated.

"He wants to kill you himself."

"Why does he want me dead?"

"I don't know! Can't you see I'm bleedin' here?" the kid cried out.

"I noticed."

Conwright jammed the gun under his jaw.

Tears welled in the boy's eyes, sweat beaded on his forehead. He shook uncontrollably. Conwright had to get him to talk before he passed out.

"Did Solly put you up to this?"

The kid looked utterly bewildered.

"Solly?" Conwright repeated. "Was it Solly?"

"Who the shit's Solly? Dude told me his name was Hanson."

"Hanson?" Conwright couldn't remember anyone named Hanson from his past. Probably an alias.

"Yeah, Hanson. That's all the fuck I know, man. He set the whole thing up. And, right now, I wish to hell I never met the stupid—"

"So, you met him? What did the guy look like?"

"What? I don't know. Little guy, like an accountant or something."

"Dark hair?"

"No hair. The dude was bald."

Not Solly, then. Who could this be?

He pressed the gun deeper under the punk's chin—

"Wait! Wait! No—"

—and put a bullet straight up through his brain.

Conwright stood, wiping blood from his face with the back of his hand. "Tough business for rookies, kid." He tossed the gun to the floor.

He got dressed, pulled the Bernadelli from its holster, and sat in the chair opposite Cartanza's corpse.

And waited.

* * *

Conwright pointed his Bernadelli directly into the man's face. Hanson, or whatever his true name was, had strolled into the room like he owned the place, his face beaming. But the smile instantly dissolved when he saw the kid dead on the floor and Conwright sitting in the chair, holding a gun.

"Never send a child to do your dirty work," Conwright said.

The man glared at Conwright, hatred and malice in his eyes. The kid was right. He was a puny, balding guy who looked everything in the world like an accountant, someone who hovered over a desk for much of his life crunching numbers and perusing spreadsheets.

"You're Hanson?"

The man said nothing.

"Why do you want to kill me?"

"You killed my fiancée."

"I've killed many people."

"Josephine Hunnicutt."

Conwright couldn't place the name. It must have been a hit, not one of his "pleasure" kills, for Hanson to attach him to the killing. He hadn't performed hits on many women over the years. Probably not a mob thing. More likely a jealous lover or ex-husband. But he was always better at faces than names. If he had a photo—

"She was to testify against Marco Gabretti, just two weeks before our wedding," Hanson said. "She witnessed his assassination of Brian Macauley, one leader of the Irish mob in Philadelphia. I guess Marco decided he didn't want her to testify ... so he hired you."

Conwright could remember the Gabretti trial. But he couldn't remember the hit, couldn't remember the woman at all. Was his memory getting that bad?

"You bastard, you don't even remember her!" Hanson vibrated with anger, clenching his fists at his sides.

"How long ago was this?"

"Nine years."

"Well, there you go! You can't expect me to remember that far back."

"You destroyed me. Took away the only love I've ever known."

"Nothing personal, I assure you. Strictly business."

Hanson's face reddened; a vein throbbed on his forehead. "You *killed* her! Of course it was personal!"

Conwright shrugged. "That's what I'm paid to do. Let me remind you, you arranged to pay me to kill. You paid the weasel on the floor over there to kill. You're no different. You have no moral high ground."

"I'm nothing like you. I despise you, you son of a bitch. I want to see you die in the worst possible fashion. Slowly. Painfully. And then I hope you roast in Hell."

Conwright shrugged again. "Tell me if I have this straight. You're a bookkeeper for the Jersey mob, and the boys told you to fund a hit on Cartanza, right?"

Hanson said nothing.

"So, you called Solly Ventura and asked for me specifically. I don't know how you figured out Solly was my liaison—"

Hanson grinned. "I have my connections. Took me years to develop them, years to track you down."

Conwright nodded. "But, once you contracted with Solly to have me hit Cartanza, you then contracted with the kid to take me out."

"No, not take you out. I wanted that opportunity."

"Do I have the story straight?"

"Think you're smart, don't you? You're not so smart."

Conwright nodded again. "I was a little sloppy this time around, I'll admit. And my gut told me something was screwy with this setup. But I never figured on you."

"So, I assume you're going to kill me now," Hanson said. He crossed his arms, glaring at Conwright. "It will bring you no satisfaction, you know."

Conwright smiled. He stood, felt a twinge of pain in his lower back again, but the pain had lessened. Maybe he was getting older, but he was still resilient.

"You clearly misunderstand me," he said. "This is a business. I'm a businessman. I don't kill unless I'm paid to do so. There is no profit in killing you." He moved closer to Hanson, making circles with the gun in his hand. "Oh, I did kill one man who refused to pay me, refused to honor our contract. Thoroughly unprofessional. I viewed it as writing off a bad debt."

Hanson's eyes never left Conwright's face. He remained silent. Conwright sensed the hatred growing like a parasite in the man's soul.

"I've killed in self-defense," Conwright continued. He took another step closer to Hanson.

"Is that why you killed the kid? In self-defense?"

"No, he was part of the contract. You paid me to take him out, same as the others. Unfortunately, your boy took them out before I had a chance, even Cartanza." Conwright sighed. "So, you owe me ten thousand, for Barcola and the kid."

"Well, I'm not part of the contract, correct?"

"True."

"And since I'm not foolish enough to attack you while you're pointing a gun in my face, I'm not an immediate threat to your life."

"Not immediate, no."

"So, you cannot kill me in self-defense."

"Right again. I have no intention of killing you. By the way, are you right-handed?"

"What?"

"Are you right-handed? It's not a tough question. Most people are right-handed. I was just wondering if you are."

"I'm right-handed, yes. But—"

Conwright thrust his Bernadelli into Hanson's right shoulder, angling the barrel up under the armpit, and rapidly pulled the trigger four times, exploding muscle, tendons, nerves, and cartilage, shattering the rotator cuff and the head of the humerus.

Hanson dropped to the floor, screeching like a skewered pig.

"Extensive corrective surgery and you'll eventually regain some use of that arm," Conwright said. "A little physical and occupational therapy, you may be able to hold a cup of coffee. Someday."

Hanson's eyes, just a moment before brimming with hatred, were now wide with fear and agony.

Conwright crouched next to him. "My advice. Drop it. You're still alive. Cherish what you have while you have it. This hatred will only consume you."

"Bastard," Hanson hissed.

"Now see, you still haven't learned the lesson here. Just remember that other parts of your body can take a bullet without killing you. Other parts can be hacked off or blown away. Please keep this in mind if you harbor any thoughts of striking out at me again. Oh, and don't forget, you owe me ten grand."

As Hanson writhed on the floor, Conwright used the kid's cell phone and anonymously reported a shooting to the police. He pocketed the phone; he'd dump it later. He also picked up the kid's gun to dispose of. Then he walked out the front door of the house.

Conwright knew, as he always knew, that he would have to watch his back.

VINDICTIVE

"You see, this is a pistol-grip mini-crossbow with an eighty-pound pull," Flash Conwright said. He turned the weapon over in his hand, admiring it. "Great for intimate work, if you know what I mean. I'm getting bored with guns. No sport, no challenge. Too messy, if you think about it."

The naked woman sitting cross-legged on the floor whimpered. Conwright had forced the woman into that position to keep her from standing and running. They were in an abandoned warehouse in a desolate section of Chicago, near the river. Refuse and abandoned furniture littered the building, and he could smell the mildew and wet-dog odor that permeated the place. To Conwright, there was a certain comfort in the musty air, in the atmosphere's closeness, like a blanket. And, of course, the darkness hid so much. There was a comfort in that, too.

She would scream. They always scream. The men, not so much. They often seemed resolute in their fate, some even welcoming it. But he knew she would scream. No one would hear her from outside the warehouse, however. Other than a few homeless people sleeping down by the docks, nobody else. So, her screaming would be meaningless. More irritating than anything. Maybe he should duct tape a sock in her mouth. Nah. What's the fun in that?

An attractive brunette with short-cropped hair, her copious makeup ran with her tears. A slim figure. Large, artificial breasts. Conwright understood everything about her was artificial. *Not bad-looking, but not my type. And I'm definitely not hers.* He could, however, understand why she attracted the boys.

"Please don't kill me," she said.

"Don't get me wrong. I love guns. A sweet Italian Bernadelli. One of my favorites. A few Berettas. Glocks. Tauruses. I even own an AK-47. Talk about messy. I'd never use that thing on the job, but it's a beautiful weapon. I have a large gun collection, all purchased legally. Not by me, of course. Background checks? What the hell are those? I'm so far off the grid, none of those guns can be traced to me."

"Please don't kill me," the woman repeated. She began to sob.

"But I love the crossbow, especially in my line of work. Like this right here, just you and me, conversing. I like to get close to my work. Far more fun, don't you think?"

"Why are you doing this?"

"Well, you and I know you're a pedophile. A murderer of young boys. I know, I know. Female pedophiles are rare, right? Probably why you got off. Having money and a powerful defense attorney didn't hurt. Victoria Wainscott, one rich bitch."

"I'm innocent. I never did anything to those boys."

"Short of seducing and killing them. What was the oldest? Fourteen? Barely into puberty. Pathetic. How many did you kill? Even the cops don't know."

"Please," she begged. Tears welled in her eyes.

"See, that one boy, Billy McPatrick? He was the grandson of someone you don't want to mess with. You probably didn't know that, did you? His grandfather hired me, an old friend of mine. Frankie Culbert. The old guy still has balls, even though he's no longer active in the Irish mob. Anyway, he's fronting the money. I think he hoped you'd get off because prison would be too easy on you."

"You don't understand."

"I understand plenty."

"It's a sickness," she said. She sniffed, wiped away tears with the back of her hand. "I couldn't help it. It's a sickness. I need help."

"I've got the help you need right here," Conwright said. He patted the crossbow and winked at her. "We're going to have some fun."

She sobbed. "I don't want to die. It's not fair. I never meant to be this way. It's a disease. You don't need to kill me. I can disappear. No one will see me again."

"Well, lady, you're right about disappearing. I'll take care of that for you."

"Look, I have money. What do you want? Whatever he's paying you, I can double it. Triple it. Whatever you want."

Conwright shook his head. "It's not about the money, lady. It's about a scumbag rich woman who tortured and killed little boys."

He shot a bolt into her groin.

The woman howled, doubling over in instant, searing agony.

"Nothing like a perforated uterus to ground you in reality," Conwright said. He loaded another bolt into the crossbow. "I know, cliché. Poetic justice. Eye for an eye, yada yada."

Her demeanor abruptly changed, as if someone threw a switch in her head. Her eyes turned to him, and he could sense the pure evil lurking behind them, her true self finally revealed. It was nothing new to Conwright. He'd seen so many similar transformations in the past. Evil had a familiar face, despite the mask it wore.

"I swear to God," she snarled. "You kill me now, I swear, I'll haunt you the rest of your life. You'll never be rid of me."

"How cliché." Conwright grinned. "You can't do better than that?"

"You'll never be rid of me," she repeated.

"I'm rid of you now, you sick bitch."

And shot a bolt into her right eye.

* * *

Conwright met with Solly Ventura at Arturo's in downtown Philadelphia, in a back-corner booth. Solly had linguini. Conwright had chicken parm. Solomon Ventura was Conwright's liaison, the guy who handled the transactions and set up all the jobs. The man was smart, had the connections, and knew how to deal. And he kept his best hitman under the radar. Conwright relished the relationship.

"Arturo outdid himself this time," Conwright said. "This parmigiana is the best I've ever eaten."

"You should taste his gnocchi. Made fresh every day. Blow your balls off."

Solly sipped his Chianti. Conwright was a Merlot man—well, if he didn't have a bourbon straight up. He swirled the wine in his glass. "So, how are the wife and kids?"

"All in good health. Thanks for askin'. Janie wants to go to Italy. One of those cruise deals. I don't know. I ain't much for boats."

"It'd do you good, Solly. Fresh sea air. Purge those sinuses. Get some relaxation."

"Screw the sea air. And I ain't got time to relax. You know this business, Flash. If you ain't on your toes, you're in the ground."

Solly sipped his wine again and then leaned forward over the table. "So, how did it go in Chicago?"

"It was fun, as usual."

"No problems?"

"Nope. In and out, done and clean. The client should be satisfied."

"Maybe even elated," Solly said. "I already have the next job lined up. Senator Fulbright."

"You're kidding."

"Nope. And, in this case, you don't need to know who hired the hit. You know, political ramifications. Big money, though. Big, big money. You can take a real vacation afterward. You've always wanted to go to Oahu, sip some pineapple shit."

"Hula girls. You bet."

After his arrest for "mishandling" government funds and embezzlement, Senator Fulbright was indicted and forced to resign from office—only to run again six years later. The idiots in the state re-elected him. Conwright would have taken the job pro bono, he hated the man so much. First, there were criminals. Further up the food chain, politicians. Conwright despised politicians.

"I honestly look forward to it," he said.

Solly nodded. "I'll get ya the details, get the ball rollin'. You know, you really should try the gnocchi next time we're here. Magnifico!"

* * *

Fulbright slept in a recliner in his den, snoring like a freight train, illuminated by a television facing the chair. Conwright had checked—Fulbright's wife slept in an upstairs bedroom. No children. Just the two of them in the house.

The large-screen TV displayed a CNN report on a terrorist attack that had occurred in San Francisco earlier that day. Fifty-two dead in a pipe-bomb attack at a megaplex movie theater. All three terrorists were killed at the scene. Conwright watched for a moment, shaking his head. If Homeland Security would hire him, he could take out terrorists, with the proper intel, before these attacks occurred. Above the law, of course, but he could use his considerable skills for a patriotic purpose, a higher purpose. He would be far more effective than law enforcement castrated by political correctness. *Pipe bombs*, Conwright thought. *Maybe the government needs stricter plumbing laws. Better background checks at Home Depot.*

He glanced at the old man in the chair and then turned to the massive bookcase set in the wall to his right. Shelves of Hemingway, Fitzgerald, Steinbeck, Salinger, Faulkner, and other names he recognized, undeniably classics. Conwright pulled down a copy of *A Farewell to Arms*, opened it. A signed first edition. What, worth thousands? He replaced it on the shelf and took down *The Great Gatsby*. Another signed first edition. He put it back on the shelf and then noticed five other copies of the same edition. Probably all signed first editions. He didn't doubt that *all* the books in the library were first editions, likely worth millions. *All paid for with tax dollars*, he thought. *Or rich lobbyists.* He looked back at Fulbright snoring in the recliner. Conwright shook his head.

He approached Fulbright from behind, pulling from his sleeve a thin stiletto secreted there. He preferred using a garrote, to watch the man thrash, unable to breathe as the wire bit into his neck. But, aware the man's wife slept upstairs, Conwright decided to dispatch the man quietly. A quick insertion of the blade through Fulbright's temple and a twist of the knife through the frontal and temporal lobes would do the trick.

He then noticed a pinpoint of light to the left of the TV, in the corner's darkness. The light seemed at first a reflection, maybe caused by a passing car on the street outside. But the room was in the basement with no windows. He stared at the light. It seemed at a great distance, like the headlight of an approaching train. Yet the pinpoint of light, now gradually expanding, also seemed to be in the room. Were his eyes playing a trick on him?

What the hell ...

The light slowly morphed into a gray, luminous form. Little more than a blob about the size of a basketball, hovering in the corner, stretching and bulging until nondescript arms and legs formed, followed by what could only be a head.

It was a little boy, Conwright realized. Eight or nine years old. But not quite a boy. The eyes were a dark blue, rimmed with violet. No, violet rimmed with blue, he couldn't be sure. The eyes had no pupils. The facial features seemed to shift and slide, to be in constant flux.

Conwright stood stock-still, more out of uncertainty than fear.

Is that the McPatrick kid?

The thing, translucent and somehow incomplete, floated above the hardwood floor. He could see the bookcase behind the specter, could see the Hemingways and Fitzgeralds through its center. There was something grotesque, something ... off ... about the boy.

Of course it's off, numbnuts. Whatever it is, it just appeared out of nowhere. And it's clearly not human.

Conwright didn't believe in ghosts. Didn't believe in anything paranormal. All bunk, the product of feeble or diseased minds.

Yet here it was in front of him. And he was of sound mind. At least, he always assumed he was.

"You're not real," he whispered.

The face rippled, shifted. Changed. Hardly human at all, the face gradually became more distinct, more recognizable. The thing tilted its head and smiled, revealing reptilian teeth.

Conwright stepped back.

The face of Victoria Wainscott. Distorted, emaciated, and gray, but her.

The face of a pedophile on a child.

"You're not real," he repeated, this time aloud.

Conwright backed away from the chair as the entity floated toward him. He didn't know what this was, and he didn't like unknowns. Unknowns could always fuck you over.

The thing seemed to laugh, but there was no sound from its bloodless lips.

He backed out of the room, closing the door behind him, fully expecting the specter to materialize in the hallway next to him. But nothing happened. He could only hear the soft snore of Fulbright's wife on the next floor.

* * *

Conwright did indeed enjoy the gnocchi at Arturo's. He did, however, retain his balls.

"I can get one of the other boys to take out Fulbright, no sweat," Solly said. "So, what the hell happened? I think this was the first time you missed a mark."

He didn't know how to answer him. Tell Solly he'd seen a ghost? The ghost of a woman he'd snuffed and now haunted him? No, he couldn't do that. But he couldn't explain it otherwise.

Conwright shook his head. "I had a bad vibe in there, in that room. Fulbright was sleeping in the chair, and I was ready to take him out. But something was off."

"Such as?"

Conwright sighed, shook his head again. "I don't know. I have to follow my intuition, and I just knew I had to get out of that room."

A lame excuse, but the best he could do.

Solly stared at him for a moment and then leaned across the table. "Look, I get the intuition thing."

"Yeah."

"But a job is a job."

* * *

A week later, Solly offered Conwright a low-profile job, a typical case of a pissed-off husband and cheating wife, Jack and Maureen Madison. Usually, with these jobs, Conwright wanted to off both parties, just for spite, just because they were so irritating. But, of course, there was no money in that.

He watched the Madison house for a week, watched Maureen's boyfriend come and go while her husband was on a job assignment in Pasadena. He'd seen the woman several times outside the house, grabbing the newspaper at the end of the driveway, a frumpy homemaker that he thought would have no appeal at all for her latest lothario. But it takes all kinds.

When he was ready to finish the job, Conwright waited one night until the boyfriend left from his latest rendezvous. He then swiftly approached the house, pulled on a ski mask and latex gloves, and quietly entered the house through a back window using a glass cutter. Her husband had the perfect alibi in California, and she likely had her lover's semen plastered in her vagina—the boyfriend would be the prime suspect. The police would never even consider a hitman. At worst, they would think it was a home invasion gone bad after he tossed the place.

When he entered the living room, she stood looking out the window. She wore a sheer nightgown, hiding nothing. She must have heard him.

"Phil, didn't have enough?"

She turned around, and her smile dissolved.

Conwright unsheathed his Schrade Guthook Skinner knife. He had no intention of gutting her, although the thought had occurred to him. Unfortunately, it would have been too much fun and would throw suspicion off the boyfriend. He would merely slit her throat.

He thought she would scream. But no.

"Oh my God," she whispered, taking a step backward.

As he approached her, twirling the knife, she slipped and fell to the floor on her back, scrambling away from him like a crab. Her eyes bulged with horror. She then screamed and pointed at him.

But not at him.

He slowly turned.

Behind him was a massive, limbless figure, sluglike and bloated, yet tall and reaching just below the ceiling. The thing's mottled flesh—if it could be called flesh—was leprous and moist. A face, a misshapen skull, floated in the goo, eyeless with cavernous sockets. But the mouth ... the mouth swarmed with an undulating mass of tentacles, a Lovecraftian nightmare.

Conwright then felt the frigid air emanating from the specter, could feel the almost palpable hatred. He instinctively slashed at the figure with the knife, but the blade slid through the vaporous entity with no effect.

Maureen Madison managed to stand and ran screaming from the room.

"You don't scare me," Conwright said. "You can put on any costume you want. A pissed-off leprechaun. A ravenous unicorn. My ex-wife. Even the Devil himself. I don't care. You can't scare me."

The skull then melted like candle wax, the tentacles dripping and dissolving in air. He could then smell the stench, the overwhelming essence of putrid death.

And the melting skull became Victoria Wainscott.

"What do you want?" Conwright said to the specter. He stood in front of it, looking directly into its transparent face. "Are you going to ruin all my jobs? That the idea? Is that all this is?"

The ghost reached for him, and he backed away.

"You don't scare me."

He heard sirens in the distance. Maureen had probably gone to a neighbor and called 911.

Conwright turned away from the specter, intending to slip out the back door before the police arrived.

He looked back over his shoulder.

The ghost was silently laughing, but did not follow him.

* * *

"Flash, it's a total fuckup! The woman gave a full report to the police, gave them a pretty accurate description of you. Thank God you wore the mask."

Solly was angry. Angrier than Conwright had ever seen his old friend.

"The husband is super pissed off," Solly continued. "And what was that shit she said about some monster in the room?"

"No idea." Anyway, no idea that he wanted to express. "I didn't see anything. Just her running from the room."

"Well, we can forget about getting the fee. How could you screw up a simple domestic contract?"

Conwright shrugged. "Sorry. That intuition thing again." No way was he going to say anything about ghosts.

"Look, I'm worried about you, Flash. If you're arrested ... well, you have ties to the organization. We'd have to take *you* out. C'mon, what's goin' on with you? This isn't like you at all."

"What can I say, Solly? When something seems wrong ..."

Solly sighed, shook his head. "How 'bout you take some time off 'til you sort things out."

* * *

This has to end, Conwright thought. He had no idea why, but he clearly had to return to Chicago, to the warehouse where he ended Victoria Wainscott's miserable life. Back to where it began. Back to where she placed the curse on him. None of this boogety-boogety stuff. He had no real religious beliefs at all. You're dead, then you're dead. That simple. You're here, then you're not.

This was different.

He stood alone in the rundown warehouse. His flashlight illuminated the stains of her blood that had soaked into the concrete floor. Victoria's body—at least what remained of her—was at the bottom of Lake Michigan, tethered to cinder blocks. He imagined her covered with lampreys.

"Where are you, you vindictive bitch?" he said to the silence. "Show yourself. I know you're here."

Nothing. Just the sound of dripping water echoing from somewhere in the dark, dank building.

He sat on the floor. Waited. Maybe this was a mistake, he thought. What did he expect to do if she confronted him again? He truly did not know. There was no plan, no strategy. Maybe he was mistaken. What did she want from him? Was she cursed to follow him forever, to foil every aspect of his life? Was she following him everywhere, only manifesting when he was on the job? Was she here *now*? Perhaps she wasn't here at all. Could she just be in his mind? No, that couldn't be it.

Why did she never speak to him? Were there regulations and policies for the dead? Restrictions? A rulebook somewhere? *Protocol for the Dead*. Was she not permitted to speak? Who knew? None of it made sense.

How do you do a hit on a ghost?

Conwright must have fallen asleep, for he abruptly awoke, conscious of the frigid air around him, aware of a slight movement nearby. No sound, but something shifting in the darkness, something low to the floor.

Victoria Wainscott congealed from the concrete, taking shape as if unfolding and developing from the floor itself. At first, the specter seemed embryonic, taking form as if in some monstrous womb. The arms appeared on an expanding torso, the legs extended, and a bulbous head grew on the stump of a neck. The thing stretched its invisible spine, becoming erect. Its fiery-violet eyes snapped open. The full figure then floated before him, grinning. She manifested as herself this time. No more games, he assumed. No more costumes.

"Good to see you again, Victoria," he said.

The face showed confusion, hesitation.

"I keep telling you I'm not afraid of you," Conwright said. "By the way, I would have done you for free, just for the satisfaction. I'd put you down again. Gladly. Maybe even with a little more inventiveness this time. Have a little more fun. Fun for me, anyway. Not so much fun for you. I can think of several power tools that would make things interesting."

The ghost tilted its head, as if inquisitive. It smiled, grotesquely wider than humanly possible and with far more teeth.

Conwright wanted to hear the thing speak, just once. What did she have to say?

She floated closer to him, radiating hatred now.

"You have no power over me. You can't harm me. You never could. I realize that now. You're just an amusement-park, ghost-house spook. A cheap, carny apparition. A sheet on a string to scare the little kids."

Victoria Wainscott's smile became a silent growl, the eyes a pulsating, ice-cold blue. She reached for him, as if to strangle him.

Conwright smiled, nodded. "Come on, then. Do your worst."

Wainscott rushed toward him, arms outstretched, emanating a cold like Conwright had never felt before. But he did not flinch. The specter passed straight through him, a mere vapor, not harming him at all.

He turned. The Wainscott entity stared at him, as if waiting for something. Bewildered.

"Are we done here?" he said.

Wainscott rushed him again, with the same result. She stood in the shadows, staring at him for a moment, confused. She moved toward him. Hesitated. Backed away this time, shaking her head. Was that fear in her eyes?

Conwright laughed.

Wainscott vanished.

* * *

Senator Fulbright was appropriately dead this time. A screwdriver protruded from his temple, a trickle of blood down his cheek. His eyes were wide with horror.

Solly had given Conwright the Fulbright contract again, to make amends. He did not fail this time.

The ghost swayed in a corner of the living room, looking bored out of whatever mind it had. If it could twiddle its thumbs, it would.

"Thanks for the help," Conwright said. "Always a pleasure to work with you, Victoria."

He chuckled. Tipped an imaginary hat in her direction.

"You know, now that we're best of pals—and you're clearly my Number One Fan—I think I'll start calling you Vicky. What do you think?"

The ghost rolled its eyes, and the face transformed into one of utter disgust. Then she blinked and promptly vanished.

Victoria had become his unwitting—and certainly unwilling—accomplice. The ghost could do nothing to frighten or deter Conwright. If anything, her appearance had made his work easier. Senator Fulbright had pissed his pants when the ghost came swirling into the room. The man didn't even see Conwright behind him until it was too late.

Perhaps her damnation was indeed to follow him around, perpetually frustrated, as he continued his business uninterrupted. He liked to think this was her hell—and well-deserved. Several times, she didn't even attempt to be frightening, just manifested in the rooms as Conwright finished the jobs. Ho hum.

He supposed you couldn't bore a ghost to death.

But it was fun trying.

ABOUT THE AUTHOR

Weldon Burge, a native of Delaware, is a thriller writer, editor, freelance writer, and publisher. He is the author of the suspense novel, *Harvester of Sorrow*, the first in the Ezekiel Marrs series.

Weldon's fiction has appeared in *Suspense Magazine*, *Futures Mysterious Anthology Magazine*, *Grim Graffiti*, *The Edge: Tales of Suspense*, *Alienskin*, *Glassfire Magazine*, *Out & About* (a Delaware magazine), and many other publications. His stories have appeared in many anthologies, including *The Best of the Horror Society*, *Pellucid Lunacy: An Anthology of Psychological Horror*, *Don't Tread on Me: Tales of Revenge and Retribution*, *A Plague of Shadows*, *Beach Pulp*, and *Monster Fight at the O.K. Corral*. He also frequently wrote author interviews for *Suspense Magazine*. Check out his author website at www.weldonburge.com.

Thank you for reading
TOXIC CANDY

Enjoy this book?
If so, you can make a huge difference!

Reviews are essential when it comes to garnering attention for books. If you liked these stories, I would be immensely grateful if you could spend a few minutes leaving a review on the book's Amazon page, Goodreads, Bookbub, or any other review site you prefer. Let other readers know about the stories you most enjoyed reading.

Thanks so much!

Weldon Burge

HARVESTER OF SORROW
AN EZEKIEL MARRS THRILLER

BY WELDON BURGE

"Burge's debut thriller kicks down the door and comes at you with both barrels blasting."—Ronald Malfi, Award-Winning Author of *Come With Me, December Park*, and *Floating Staircase*

"A thrilling start to what I hope will be a long-running series! A grisly and fascinating novel!"—Jeff Strand, Author of *My Pretties*

"Weldon Burge's debut Ezekiel Marrs novel, *Harvester of Sorrow*, is a masterpiece of detective fiction. I look forward to reading more Marrs cases."—Quintin Peterson, Author of *S.I.N., Guarding Shakespeare,* and *The Voynich Gambit*